Keep Up With Me?"

The dare in Leanna's eyes stirred his competitive blood. "Sweetheart, the question isn't whether or not *I* could keep up with *you*. It's whether or not I'd leave you eating my dust. I am good."

For three dances he spun, dipped and twirled her, using every intricate dance move he knew, and he knew 'em all. Leanna never missed a step. It'd been ages since he'd had a partner who could keep up with him. His breathing became unsteady and he felt a little feverish. He had a serious hankering to kiss that sassy smirk right off her lips.

Mischief sparkled in her eyes. "Did I mention my former employer's last lover was a dance instructor?"

He'd been hustled *twice* by a wet-behind-the-ears gal. He'd underestimated her abilities as a hostess and a dance partner, and he had to wonder if she had any more surprises in store for him....

Dear Reader,

Thanks for choosing Silhouette Desire, *the* place to find passionate, powerful and provocative love stories. We're starting off the month in style with Diana Palmer's *Man in Control,* a LONG, TALL TEXANS story and the author's 100th book! Congratulations, Diana, and thank you so much for each and every one of your wonderful stories.

Our continuing series DYNASTIES: THE BARONES is back this month with Anne Marie Winston's thrilling tale *Born To Be Wild.* And Cindy Gerard gives us a fabulous story about a woman who finds romance at her best friend's wedding, in *Tempting the Tycoon.* Weddings seem to be the place to meet a romantic partner (note to self: get invited to more weddings), as we find in Shawna Delacorte's *Having the Best Man's Baby.*

Also this month, Kathie DeNosky is back with another title in her ongoing ranching series—don't miss *Lonetree Ranchers: Morgan* and watch for the final story in this trilogy coming in December. Finally, welcome back the wonderful Emilie Rose with *Cowboy's Million-Dollar Secret,* a fantastic story about a man who inherits much more than he ever expected.

More passion to you!

Melissa Jeglinski

Melissa Jeglinski
Senior Editor
Silhouette Desire

Please address questions and book requests to:
Silhouette Reader Service
U.S.: 3010 Walden Ave., P.O. Box 1325, Buffalo, NY 14269
Canadian: P.O. Box 609, Fort Erie, Ont. L2A 5X3

Cowboy's Million-Dollar Secret

EMILIE ROSE

Published by Silhouette Books

America's Publisher of Contemporary Romance

To Kim Nadelson, my editor.
I couldn't do this without you.

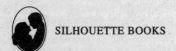 SILHOUETTE BOOKS

ISBN 0-373-76542-8

COWBOY'S MILLION-DOLLAR SECRET

Copyright © 2003 by Emilie Rose Cunningham

This edition published by arrangement with Harlequin Books S.A.

® and TM are trademarks of Harlequin Books S.A., used under license.
Trademarks indicated with ® are registered in the United States Patent
and Trademark Office, the Canadian Trade Marks Office and in other
countries.

Visit Silhouette at www.eHarlequin.com

Printed in U.S.A.

Books by Emilie Rose

Silhouette Desire

Expecting Brand's Baby #1463
The Cowboy's Baby Bargain #1511
The Cowboy's Million-Dollar Secret #1542

EMILIE ROSE

lives in North Carolina with her college-sweetheart husband and four sons. This bestselling author's love for romance novels developed when she was twelve years old and her mother hid them under sofa cushions each time Emilie entered the room. Emilie grew up riding and showing horses. She's a devoted baseball mom during the season and can usually be found in the bleachers watching one of her sons play. Her hobbies include quilting, cooking (especially cheesecake) and anything cowboy. Her favorite TV shows include Discovery Channel's medical programs, *ER, CSI* and *Boston Public*. Emilie's a country music fan because there's an entire book in nearly every song.

Emilie loves to hear from her readers and can be reached at P.O. Box 20145, Raleigh, NC 27619 or at http://www.EmilieRose.com.

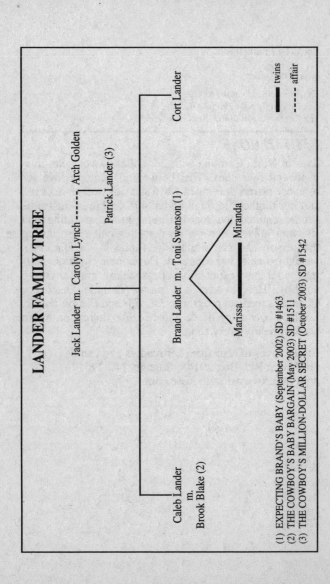

LANDER FAMILY TREE

Jack Lander m. Carolyn Lynch ----- Arch Golden

Caleb Lander
m.
Brook Blake (2)

Patrick Lander (3)

Brand Lander m. Toni Swenson (1)

Cort Lander

Marissa   Miranda

———— twins
----- affair

(1) EXPECTING BRAND'S BABY (September 2002) SD #1463
(2) THE COWBOY'S BABY BARGAIN (May 2003) SD #1511
(3) THE COWBOY'S MILLION-DOLLAR SECRET (October 2003) SD #1542

One

One cowboy.

One final request.

Fifteen million dollars.

Leanna Jensen smiled and congratulated herself on finding a way to tie all three into a neat package. "You won't regret giving me the job, Ms. Lander."

"Call me Brooke. If you'll follow me into the kitchen I'll introduce you to my brother-in-law." Leanna's new boss led the way across the expansive common room, calling over her shoulder, "I forgot to mention when we spoke on the phone that Patrick will be managing the dude ranch while my husband and I are away."

Leanna's steps faltered. She hadn't expected to meet the star player of her adolescent daydreams so soon. Would he measure up to her high expectations or disappoint her like every other man? "Patrick is here? Now?"

"In the flesh." The deep voice drew her gaze to the cowboy already occupying the spacious dude ranch dine-in kitchen. Slumped over a glass of iced tea at the end of the long pine table, he slowly straightened. His twinkling dark eyes and charismatic grin stole her breath.

Brooke motioned her forward. "Patrick, this is Leanna Jensen. She'll be filling in for me as hostess for the next month. Leanna, Patrick."

Pressing a hand over her leaping heart, Leanna moved farther into the room. Her feet practically floated above the floor. She'd waited nine years to meet the son Carolyn Lander had described in her letters to her lover.

At thirty-six, the man unfolding inch by muscular inch in front of her was ten times more potent than the lean and lanky sixteen-year-old he'd been in the last photo Arch had received.

"I-it's n-nice to meet you." She never stuttered or stammered, but Patrick in the flesh was much more manly than she'd imagined. Taller. Broader.

Sexier. She pushed that unwelcome thought aside.

Her gaze raced over his features like a runaway roller coaster. Patrick's dark, smoldering looks were the complete opposite of his biological father's, but his classically honed features and sensuously full mouth were the same ones Arch Golden had parlayed into a fortune on the big screen. He'd left that fortune to Patrick, the son he'd never met, but had worried about up until his last breath.

The ache in her heart over losing Arch momentarily overshadowed the thrill of finally meeting his son. Perhaps once she and Patrick became friends they could curl up by a campfire and exchange stories—his exciting tales of life on a ranch, rescuing animals and fighting wildfires and hers about the incredible man who'd fathered him. She especially wanted to make sure Patrick knew that his father—*his real father*—had loved him even though the two had never met.

She hadn't been as lucky.

Squaring her shoulders, Leanna met the gaze of the man she'd driven over a thousand miles to meet, and eagerly reached for the hand he extended. She'd read so much about him in his mother's letters that meeting him was almost like meeting an old friend, and yet an old friend wouldn't make her fingers tremble.

As if he knew the unsettling effect his good looks had on her, Patrick's grin deepened, crinkling the laugh lines around his dark eyes and deepening the grooves bracketing his mouth. His warm, slightly rough grasp seemed to reach right down inside her and squeeze her already nervous stomach tighter.

Dear heavens, he was handsome. Her mouth dried and her knees wobbled.

"Hey, there. So we're gonna play house?" He waggled his dark brows and gave her a slow wink.

Her stomach bottomed out. A tiny drop of doubt threatened to rain on her parade. Was Patrick a charmer and a flirt? Surely the man she'd waited so long to meet wasn't the very type she'd spent most of her life avoiding?

"I'm going to be keeping house, not playing." Nervousness made her voice come out sterner than she'd intended. She sounded like a schoolmarm. Embarrassed, she tugged her hand free. Witty, be witty. She'd learned social repartee at her mother's knee. What was her problem?

He rolled his wide shoulders in a shrug. "'All work and no play...'"

"Is a good way to get ahead." Rats. That sounded worse than before, but her insides jangled like loose change in a jogger's pocket. She fought the urge to wring her hands, shoving her fists into her pants pockets instead. Her palm continued to tingle.

The wattage in his lady-killer grin dimmed. Leaning a hip against the table, he crossed his scuffed and dusty boots. "I can tell you're going to be a load of fun."

His sarcasm stung, like tearing a scab off a nearly healed wound. It wasn't the first time she'd heard that from a man.

He folded his arms and turned a long-suffering look toward his sister-in-law. "You and Caleb did this on purpose, didn't you?"

Brooke's eyes widened. "I don't know what you mean."

"Sure you do. You and big brother hired a strait-laced baby-sitter to keep me in line while you're off on your book tour." And he wasn't pleased.

Hurt that he'd pigeon-holed her so easily and that he obviously wasn't as thrilled to meet her as she was to meet him, Leanna clenched her teeth. "I'm a hostess, not a baby-sitter."

He shoved a lock of hair off his brow, yanked his black hat from the hook beside the back door, and parked it on his head in one smooth, choreographed move. "Right."

With his hat pulled low on his forehead, Patrick Lander looked like the real deal as far as cowboys went. She'd bet the muscles straining the shoulders of his plaid shirt and the thighs of his faded jeans hadn't come from a personal trainer, and his tanned skin looked genuine, not the result of some expensive cream. There wasn't any Hollywood in him.

Yet. She chewed her lip.

Would a multimillion-dollar inheritance change him? She certainly hoped not, because thanks to her mom, she'd already had a parade of Hollywood phonies and live-for-the-minute men in her life. What she needed now was a man she could trust, a friend to replace the one she'd lost. She hoped to find one in Arch's son.

He turned for the door, but she wasn't ready to let him go. She had a zillion questions to ask. None of which she actually *could* ask without giving too much away too soon. But she had to think of something to keep him from walking out. "Do you *need* someone to watch your every move?"

Patrick paused and slowly pivoted. An assessing light entered his eyes and then he chuckled. The sound slid over her nerve endings like the scrape of a cat's tongue. "If I did, it wouldn't be some gal half my age. I could run circles around you without breaking a sweat."

She swallowed hard. Gaining his friendship wasn't going to be as easy as she'd hoped. "How old do you think I am?"

His dark gaze fastened on her with the sharp focus of a paparazzo's zoom lens. He took in the stick-straight brown hair she'd pulled back with a barrette, her beige shirt and slacks, and her sensible shoes in a look so slow and thorough she grew warm all over.

The flash of vanity making her long for something besides her baggy traveling outfit was totally ridiculous. The last thing she wanted to be was attracted to a charmer, or worse yet, to have to dodge one's advances.

The corners of his mouth curled upward, and her stomach fluttered. Then, when his smile twisted into an irritated expression, her hopes sank.

"You can't be more than eighteen, kid. It's likely I'll end up hauling your butt out of trouble every time I turn around. Between corralling the dudes and keeping Dad from working himself to death over on our place, I won't have time. We're short-handed and there's no room for dead weight."

The "kid" comment rankled. She'd been looking after herself and her mother for as long as she could remember. Stretching up to her full height, which left her a head shorter than Patrick, she threw back her shoulders.

"I'm twenty-one. I don't need looking after, and I'll carry my share of the load. As for you running circles around me…you'll be lucky if you can keep up with me."

She bit her tongue and took a calming breath. When backed into a corner she tended to get smart-mouthed, but now was not the time to wise-off. Arguing in front of her new employer was likely to get the job offer rescinded. She glanced at Brooke.

Her new boss watched the byplay with an interested and amused expression on her face but made no comment.

Leanna forced a smile. "I came here to work, Mr. Lander, not to have fun."

"*You* might not be looking for fun, but our guests will be. From sunup to bunk-down, fun is our profession. And the name's Patrick. I don't answer to anything else except in the bedroom. And, kid—'' his lips curled in a sly, knowing smile that twisted her insides in a peculiar way ''—you and I won't ever be in the same one at the same time.''

At least they agreed on one thing. Relieved, she smiled back. ''Not unless you're pushing the vacuum.''

He didn't smile, but his lips twitched, and a spark danced in his dark eyes. She thought she detected a trace of grudging respect. ''Where are you staying?''

She blinked at his change of topic and bit the inside of her cheek. Glancing from Patrick to Brooke and back, she shrugged. ''The job description was a little unclear. Aren't accommodations part of the package?''

Brooke shook her head. ''The only staff member who lives on-site is Toby, the head trail boss.''

Patrick faced Brooke. ''Your painters will be in first thing tomorrow morning. The Double C's booked solid. She can't stay here.''

An unexpected twist, but she'd sleep in her car, if necessary. It wouldn't be the first time she made her bed in a back seat. Leanna asked, ''Painters?''

Brooke nodded and rested a hand over her stomach. ''Caleb and I are expecting. We decided to have our private quarters redecorated while we're traveling, because we didn't want the baby exposed to the paint fumes or the dust from the floor refinishers. Maria, our housekeeper, offered to keep an eye on everything, but she's been unexpectedly called away.''

Brooke crossed the room and pulled a phone book from the drawer. ''Patrick's right. We can't house you at the Double C, but there's a rooming house about ten miles from here. I'll write down the address and phone number for you—if you're still interested in the job?''

''I'm definitely interested.'' She couldn't imagine

anything more wonderful than spending the next month learning more about the Lander family. Carolyn Lander hadn't been happy in this remote section of Texas, although she'd stayed there till she died twenty years ago. But to Leanna, who'd spent years dodging paparazzi as part of her job with Arch, wide-open spaces sounded like heaven.

Besides, someone had to help Patrick deal with the devastating news she was about to deliver. And maybe, just maybe, he could fill the void Arch's death left in her life.

"In that case," Brooke continued, "I've left a thorough description of my job duties for you along with Maria's daughter's phone number." She pointed to a piece of paper pinned on the bulletin board above the counter. "She said you could call her if you had any questions. I don't think I left anything out during our tour of the facilities, but why don't you look over the list while I get the boarding house address?"

Patrick intercepted Leanna before she could reach the bulletin board. He moved so swiftly she had to put up her hands to prevent a collision. Her fingertips grazed his firm chest and a tingle jolted clear to her elbows. His cedar and citrus scent teased her senses. Disconcerted, she took a quick step back.

"Maria has her hands full with her grandkids while her daughter's recuperating from surgery. Don't bug her. You need anything, you whistle for me. Got it?" His voice was low and intimate, as if he didn't want his sister-in-law to overhear.

It didn't take a rocket scientist to figure out that Patrick didn't think she was qualified for the position of hostess. Mentally dusting off her hands, she met the challenge in his eyes.

"My former employer had a forty-room home with an in-house staff of four, along with an outside staff that varied depending on the season. I supervised them all. Guests were always coming and going. I can handle the dude ranch."

Her words had no visible effect on him, but she held her ground. Experience had taught her not to respond to intimidation.

Brooke's voice intruded on their staring match. "I'm sorry Arch Golden's death forced you to seek other employment, Leanna, but his attorney—who coincidentally used to be mine before I moved to Texas—gave you a glowing reference."

He would. Phil knew the role Leanna had played in his client's life, as well as the one she'd now been assigned to play as the executrix of Arch's estate. Sitting in Phil's office it had sounded relatively easy to fulfill her executrix duties. All she had to do was contact Patrick and tell him about his real father and his inheritance *before* the press crashed down on him with the news.

Arch's last request was a little more complicated. He'd asked her to explain to Patrick that although he'd never tried to contact his son, he had loved him. In return, Arch had promised her enough money to finish college and keep her mother in rehab. She would have agreed without the promise of money, because the stories Carolyn had written about Patrick's boyhood escapades had whetted her appetite for adventure—cowboy-style.

Patrick Lander, according to his mother, was a man of the land and good with animals and children. He had a family history—something Leanna sorely lacked—and he'd lived in the same place since birth.

Compared to her life, his sounded like a fairy-tale, and compared to the court jesters she'd dated, he sounded like King Arthur. The tales of his gallantry had certainly spoiled her for every man she'd met.

"You worked for a movie star?" Patrick stepped back, looking and sounding repulsed rather than impressed, the way most people were by her former employer.

She sighed. Her friendship apparently didn't rank high on his list of things to accomplish today. Well, tomorrow was another day, as Scarlett had said. "Yes, but managing staff and making guests comfortable, whether it's paying customers or just friends dropping in, are universal skills."

"Right."

She'd never known one word could carry so much sarcasm, and she'd lived with an actor for the last six years. Pivoting on his worn-down boot heel, her quarry opened the back door but paused in the threshold. "Brooke, tell Caleb I'll catch up with him later."

"Patrick." Brooke hurried across the kitchen and stopped him with a hand on his arm. "I know the extra work is going to be tough on you while we're away, and I want you to know how much Caleb and I appreciate you allowing us this time together before the baby comes."

A flush darkened Patrick's neck and cheekbones. Looking decidedly uncomfortable, he shifted from one boot to the other. "You haven't been married to my brother long enough to know there's nothing I won't do for family."

Leanna's heart soared with hope. Family loyalty. She'd sell her soul for it. Oh, how she longed to be a part of a big clan like the Landers'. She crossed her fingers and said a prayer that her announcement wouldn't test Patrick's family bonds.

Brooke went up on tiptoe to plant a kiss on Patrick's flushed cheek. "Well, this is certainly above and beyond the call of duty. Thank you."

His blush intensified. "No big deal. Caleb would do the same for me." He ducked out quickly and closed the door.

What was Caleb thinking to hire a kid to baby-sit him?

All right, Patrick admitted as he crossed the yard, maybe his past escapades might lead some to think he needed a watchdog. But a kid? Okay, so Leanna wasn't exactly a kid, but she was too damned young to have the experience necessary to handle the huge responsibility of hostess on a dude ranch during peak season no matter what she said.

He glanced back over his shoulder and there she stood, framed in the kitchen window. Big hazel eyes. A pouty mouth. Curves a man would need a road map to get around. Attraction was a distraction he didn't need right now.

It didn't help that she had a sense of humor. He chuckled. Vacuum. Right. He'd been trying to warn her off and she'd put him in his place.

He made a beeline for the barn to escape the sun baking his hide and spotted a station wagon parked near his truck. Probably *hers,* judging by the out-of-state tags.

Slowing his steps, he looked through the windows. Had she packed everything she owned into the back of her wagon? You'd think the gal didn't have a home to return to. He shook his head and shrugged off the questions piling up in his brain. Not his problem. She'd hostess awhile and then haul her load back to California. End of story.

The barn was dark, but still hotter than Hades, and the humidity was thick enough to drown in. The windows to the tack room were open, but that didn't matter since not even a hint of a breeze stirred the stagnant air. He swiped the sweat from his brow, snatched up the phone and punched in his home number. His father picked up.

"What're you doing, Pop?"

"Same damned thing I was doing last time you called."

"Well, take a break and get out of the heat. It's hotter than the devil's hearth today."

"You'd be more likely to know about the devil than most of us, I reckon, but I ain't got time for lollygaggin'."

"And I don't have time to haul you to the clinic for heat stroke. It's your turn to fix lunch. Why don't you head inside and make us a couple of sandwiches and a cold drink. I'm on my way."

Patrick hung up on his father's grumbling and hiked toward his pickup.

Stubborn ol' coot. His father was aging right before his eyes. The workload was too heavy for just the two of them, but his dad was as obstinate as a mule about hiring anyone to help. Said money was too tight to squeeze in another salary. Swore he'd pick up any slack his sons' marriages had created.

Not without killing himself. Maybe both of them.

Patrick couldn't refuse his brother's request to manage the dude ranch while he and Brooke were away, but he sure didn't know how he'd juggle the family spread and the Double C Dude Ranch and keep his father from working too hard at the same time. But he would. Dammit, he would.

It meant temporarily giving up poker, beer and women until Caleb returned, but he could handle hard work and celibacy for a short spell without going insane. Probably.

He'd call Caleb later and ask him about those college kids he'd turned away. Hiring them would be another bone of contention between him and his father, but what was one more? It seemed these days he and Pop fought about everything.

He jerked to a stop at the sight of a set of prime hind quarters bent over the open hood of the station wagon. Leanna might wear baggy clothes, but nothing could conceal those curves. Not to a man with eyes in his head, anyway. He tamped down his reaction and reminded himself that he had no time for detours.

"Problem?"

She spun around and a shy smile turned up the corners of her mouth. "The engine smelled a little hot when I arrived, but everything looks and sounds okay now."

He bit down on the urge to flex his muscles and smile back. Something in the way the Double C's newest employee looked at him made him feel ten feet tall. She was definitely too darn young for him.

So why did one shy glance from her hit him like a sucker punch in the gut?

He stifled the urge to help. This wasn't his problem, even though damsels in distress were his number-one weakness. Heck, women *period* were his weakness, but starting today, he was on a woman-free diet.

A quick check of her car's reservoir told him it held

plenty of antifreeze. The engine wasn't in danger of overheating and it sounded normal. "Pete's Garage is on the way to the Pink Palace. If you're worried, get him to take a look."

"The Pink Palace?"

In the bright sunlight he noticed the dapple of faded freckles on her nose and cheeks and the golden streaks in her light-brown hair. She was cute, in an all-American girl-next-door kind of way. He preferred women with a little more flash and a lot more experience, but heaven help the men on the spread—and him—if she ever slapped on a layer of war paint or squeezed herself into tight blue jeans.

"Penny's place. It used to be a whor—brothel."

A blush crawled up her neck and spread to her hairline. That blush was a sure sign she was out of his league. Only virgins blushed like that, and he adhered to a strict no-virgins policy. Virgin hearts broke too easily. Virgins expected a guy to be loyal, but he was his mother's son. Loyalty wasn't encoded on his DNA.

Leanna was off-limits. Taboo.

If he repeated the words often enough he might remember 'em.

"I'll be staying in a whore house?"

Aw, heck, she wasn't going to get prudish on him, was she? "Used to be one, but the sheriff closed down that side of the business years ago. It's been a rooming house all my life."

She slammed the hood and grimaced at her dirty hands.

Patrick pulled his bandanna out of his pocket and offered it to her before he could stop himself. Even good habits were hard to break. "Don't let Penny put you in room ten."

Her chin jerked up and suspicion dimmed the gold flecks in her eyes. "Why?"

"It's haunted."

Instead of looking at him like he was a couple of bales short of a trailer load, he noted a spark of interest. "You're teasing me."

"No, ma'am. Story is that one of the madam's customers wanted to take her away from her business. He proposed. She refused. He *offed* her because she loved her, ah…work more than him and he didn't want to share."

Her eyes widened, and then she beamed like he'd just handed her a winning lottery ticket. He staggered back a step. That smile of hers nearly blinded him. Leanna Jensen wasn't just cute, she was damned dazzling. Put a cork in it, Lander. He tried to shake off the unwanted attraction.

She practically danced with excitement. "Get out of here. A ghost? Really?"

He hesitated to tell her the local legend, fearing she'd misread any effort at conversation as sign of interest, but he couldn't resist the questions in her eyes. "Folks say that if you make love in room ten your partner won't be the only one with you."

Ghost stories creeped him out. He'd never had the desire to investigate the madam's story or any of the others his mother had told him on those long nights when she'd dragged him out of bed, strapped him into the car and circled the Palace time and time again. Whatever it was she thought she'd see, she'd always gone home disappointed, and he'd always crawled into bed and cowered under the covers, waiting for the nightmares her tales conjured up.

"A haunted whore house." Leanna's delighted

chuckle drew him back from his bitter childhood memories. The sound, combined with the anticipation lighting her up like a neon sign, made him wonder if she might *not* be a straitlaced stick-in-the-mud after all. His body responded in a way it shouldn't, considering he had no intention of following where it urged him to go.

"I *love* ghost stories." Her smile widened and mischief made the gold flecks in her eyes sparkle. Pink tinted her cheeks as she peeked at him from beneath her gold-tipped lashes. She lowered her voice. "Have you ever tested the tale? You know, to see if there's an amorous ghost?"

Too cute. Too young. Into ghosts. And testing his temporary vow of celibacy. Just his luck.

"No." He took a long stride backward, opened his truck door and put it between them.

In the past year, wily women had shanghaied two of his brothers into marriage, and while Leanna didn't seem to be the wily type, he wasn't taking any chances. Brand and Caleb were happy enough, but marriage wasn't for him. His mother hadn't had a faithful bone in her body, and as far as he could tell, he was just like her. More'n one woman had tried to put a ring around his finger—a noose around his neck, to his way of thinking—but he wasn't promising forever to anybody. He'd disappointed enough people in his life.

"Penny can probably tell you more about it. Don't forget to stop by Pete's. See you tomorrow." He climbed into the cab and backed out of the space before he did something stupid like ask her to dinner.

Two

Leanna's Buick roared like an expensive sports car. It wasn't a good sign since the station wagon wasn't moving—unless you counted the slight backward roll.

She pursed her lips and pressed the gas pedal once again. Nothing. The gauges gave no indication of distress, but something was definitely wrong with her car. Taking her foot off the brake, she coasted backward off the road and onto the grassy verge and then turned off the engine. Heat immediately filled the interior, forcing her to roll down the windows while she debated her options.

Arch's chauffeur had walked her though filling the assorted fluid tanks before she'd left Carlsbad, but that was the extent of her knowledge about the inner workings of a car. She pulled the latch and climbed out to take another look beneath the hood, but to her inexperienced eye everything appeared as it should.

Sweat plastered her clothes to her body within minutes. She nibbled a nail. Her car had to be repaired. One of the most important lessons she'd learned growing up was that you had to have a plan B—a way to escape if a situation became ugly. It was the reason she'd saved a portion of her salary—the portion her mother's treatment didn't consume—and bought her own car a few months ago.

She stared into the distance at the heat haze wavering on the asphalt. Barbed-wire fencing stretched along either side of the road, marking dry, empty pastures. She hadn't passed another car on the six-mile stretch of road between here and the Double C Dude Ranch. If Brooke's directions were correct she was closer to the gas station and rooming house than the ranch.

As much as she loved to read about knights and heroes, she'd learned the hard way that they rarely walked off the pages of a book.

She secured the vehicle and hiked toward help.

Hot, tired, and sweat-soaked from the skin out, Leanna wasn't in the mood for bad news.

"Transmission's shot," Pete said without losing the toothpick stuck between his teeth. The man was every Hollywood cliché she'd ever seen of a small-town garage mechanic. His overalls were stained and the bill of his ball-cap faced backwards. Every third sentence he spit a stream of tobacco into a paper cup.

She daubed the sweat from her brow with Patrick's bandanna and tried to ignore the way his scent lingered on the fabric. "How much to repair the car?"

"New parts, fifteen hundred. Rebuilt, eleven. It'll take me about a week either way."

Her stomach sank. She'd destroyed all of her credit

cards after her mother's last binge, and she'd emptied her bank account paying in advance for three months' worth of her mother's rehab at the new and expensive clinic. Arch's estate had only allowed her two thousand dollars for the entire Texas trip—a portion of which she'd spent on the way here. "Rebuilt."

"Cash. Up front."

She tried not to wince, but she wouldn't receive a paycheck from the dude ranch until the end of the month. If she paid the mechanic now she wouldn't be able to afford a room at the Pink Palace. She'd barely be able to buy food. At least working at the dude ranch included most meals.

Regret pulled her gaze back to the plate glass window. Down the road, the elegant lines of a large Victorian house with a resident ghost called to her. "Can I pay you half now and half at the end of the month?"

"Don't extend credit to strangers—especially the ones with out-of-state tags."

"I'll be working at the Double C Dude Ranch."

"Ask Caleb's missus for an advance on your salary. She's a Californian, too." He made it sound like she'd come from another planet not just another state.

She made it a practice never to owe anybody anything, except Arch, and she was here to clear that debt.

Between the time she'd run away at fifteen and when Arch had found her sleeping in one of his classic cars eight months later, she'd hidden in all kinds of places. It looked like she'd have to again tonight.

She took one last wistful glance at the Palace's twin-turreted structure and vowed that one day she'd own a home with a deep front porch, window boxes and porch swings. Right now she needed a place to sleep. Reluctantly she counted out the money.

"Could you give me a ride to the Double C?"

*   *   *

Patrick found his father hunched over breakfast before sunup. The ashen tone of his skin and the tired slump of his shoulders worried him. "You have trouble sleeping again?"

"No."

A blatant lie. He'd heard his father pacing the floor because he'd also been awake thinking about the Double C's new hostess. He couldn't do her job and his, too, if she didn't measure up.

He couldn't afford to be attracted to her.

"Why don't I run you by the clinic this morning and get the doc to check your blood pressure?"

"I ain't going to the doctor. Won't get nothing but a little bottle of pills and a big bill."

"You can't put a price on your health, Pop."

"Tell that to those bandits."

The muscles in Patrick's neck knotted. They'd had this argument a dozen times. Nothing short of an ambulance would get Jack Lander to the clinic. "How about taking it easy today? The heat index is going to be up there."

"You take it easy if you want. I got work to do."

"Caleb gave me the name of a couple of college kids. I hired them to help here while I'm managing the dude ranch."

His father scowled. "Can't afford it."

"Caleb's paying me enough to cover both salaries."

"You hired your brother's rejects?"

He gritted his teeth, counted to ten and wondered if he should have his own blood pressure checked. "The kids are majoring in animal science at Tech, and they need on-the-job experience. Helping them helps us."

''Well, I ain't interested in baby-sitting greenhorns.''

Talking was a waste of breath when his father was this tetchy. ''I'm heading over to the Double C. Keith and John will be here by nine. I'll be back to get 'em started.''

Arguing with his father before his first cup of coffee guarandamnteed he'd start the day in a foul mood. Patrick headed for his truck and took out his frustrations on the gearshift during the short drive to the property next door.

The Double C had been a part of Crooked Creek until a decade ago when Caleb's first wife had nearly bankrupted them. They'd been forced to sell half the ranch to keep from losing the entire spread. The new owner had opened a dude ranch which Brooke had bought right out from under their noses a few months back. And then Caleb had married her. Worse, his brother had fallen *in love*—an affliction Patrick planned on fighting all the way to his grave.

His newest sister-in-law had crazy ideas about operating a motivational retreat. City-slickers getting in touch with their inner souls, or some such hype. Caleb had convinced her to try running a dual operation for a year, but Patrick worried that her motivational thing would take off and she'd phase out the dude ranch.

He was probably the only one who hoped she wouldn't decide to close the dude ranch portion of the Double C. His brother and his father preferred ranching, but for him working with the dudes was like summer camp—a little grit, but mostly fun. Each week brought new faces and a fresh crop of enthusiasm. It beat the heck out of riding drag and eating dust behind a herd of cattle. Besides, the dudes actually begged to do the dirty work. It left him feeling a little like Huck Finn when he pawned off his chores.

He glanced at his watch as he parked in the shade beside the barn. None of the crew was due until after lunch. Since the next batch of guests would arrive tomorrow, he'd have to work his tail off today. The sooner he started, the sooner he'd finish.

He stomped up the back porch stairs of the Double C homestead.

"Good morning."

He whipped around at Leanna's husky greeting. She lay curled in a lounge chair in the far corner of the porch with Brooke's mangy mutt Rico at her side. With her hair mussed and hanging over her shoulders, she looked soft and sleepy. *And sexy.* He slammed the door on his wayward thoughts.

"You're early. Trying to score points with the boss?"

She smiled up at him. "Would it work?"

He couldn't help but grin back. "Nope. Beating me to work makes me look bad."

She scratched the dog behind his ragged, partially chewed-off ear and cupped the mutt's face. "Rico won't tell. Will you, boy?"

You had to like a gal who'd befriend a butt-ugly dog. He dug in his pocket for his key and unlocked the door.

"Brooke said you'd give me keys and introduce me to everyone."

Evidently, Brooke and Caleb had made him social director before they'd left last night. Brooke wasn't handling mornings well in the first trimester of her pregnancy and preferred not to travel early in the morning.

"Should be a set of spares inside."

Leanna unfolded in increments as if her muscles were stiff. He thought it a little odd considering her age—or lack of age. "You look like you've been ridden hard and put up wet."

As soon as the words came out of his mouth an image formed in his mind—an image that had nothing to do with mistreating a horse. *Down boy.* He shoved open the door and motioned her to go ahead.

"Uh…no, just a strange bed. Do you mind if I make coffee?"

He followed her into the kitchen, wondering if the lack of caffeine was causing his mind to wander in the wrong direction. "Go ahead."

She searched through the cabinets looking for the fixings. Each time she reached up, the strip of skin between the waistband of her baggy pants and the hem of her loose butter-yellow T-shirt widened.

His hormones obviously realized he was fixin' to hang 'em out for a long dry spell and were already rebelling.

With enormous effort he yanked his gaze away and reached past her for the coffee. His chest brushed her shoulder. Her hip nudged his. By the way his body reacted, she might as well have jumped on the kitchen table and started a bump-and-grind strip show.

Damn, he needed coffee. And a cold shower. He shoved the can into her hands and hustled across the room before he gave in to the urge to see if her skin felt as warm and smooth as it looked.

"Thanks." Her voice sounded a little husky.

He squinted at her. Was she having as hard a time catching her breath as he was? Get your head outta the gutter and back on business, Lander. "You and Brooke handled all the paperwork yesterday?"

She scooped coffee grounds into the filter and smiled at him. "Yes, and she explained the dude ranch schedule. Guests arrive on Saturday and stay through Wednesday afternoon. The staff has Thursday and half of Friday off."

"Why're you early?"

Her cheeks looked flushed, but it was probably just a reflection of the sunrise coming through the window. "I need to familiarize myself with where everything is before we get caught up in the guests' arrival." She stretched to put up the coffee.

He caught another glimpse of skin and inhaled, but it wasn't coffee he smelled—not unless Brooke had switched to a prissy vanilla-scented brew. Suddenly it struck him that he and Leanna were the only ones in the house. Clearing his throat, he wiped a hand across his face. The bristles reminded him that in the rush to avoid another argument with his father he'd forgotten to shave.

"She gave you the uniform?"

"Yes, but she said I didn't have to wear it until tomorrow and then only for the first two days to help the guests identify me as an employee. Can you tell me where Rico's food is kept?"

"Laundry room."

She called to the dog and walked out of the room. Patrick caught himself tracking her—or rather the hip-rolling motion of her tight, round hind quarters, and shook his head. Label the gal off-limits, and danged if he didn't develop a one-track mind.

Quit thinking about her and get back to work, dammit. It wasn't like he didn't have a truckload to do. He snatched up the computer printout Caleb had left him and scanned the information about the incoming dudes. Most were families with kids, but there were a few couples and singles. He'd learned the hard way to keep his eye on the singles.

He heard the splash of coffee into a mug and turned. Leanna had returned so quietly he hadn't heard her. She lifted the pot in his direction and arched a brow. He nodded and she filled his cup.

Leaning against the counter, she asked, "Brooke said you had two brothers besides Caleb. Are you close?"

He jerked his gaze away from the freckles splashed across her nose and discovered a toe ring on her sandaled foot. Different. Sexy. Heat curled in his belly. Aw, hell, did he have to discover a foot fetish now? "As close as most, I guess."

"Do you help Caleb and Brooke with the dude ranch often?" She pursed her lips and blew on her steaming coffee, and he almost forgot her question. She'd painted her pouty mouth today. Red. Ripe. Ready.

Wrong. Man, he needed to go back home and start this day over. He rubbed the back of his neck. She'd asked him a question. What was it? "Brooke's only owned the place a few months, but Caleb and I used to help the previous owner regularly."

"You live next door with your father?"

"Yeah."

"How does he feel about you working here?"

Where was the line of questions leading, and why did he feel as if he were being interviewed? "Probably glad to have me out of his hair."

"You don't get along?"

It could take him all day to answer *that* one. "Not as good as we could. Why?"

He thought she smiled into her coffee mug. "Just curious."

"Right. If we're playing twenty questions then why're you here?"

She stilled and slowly lifted her gaze to his. "I needed a job."

"In *Texas?*" He sipped his coffee and discovered Leanna made a danged good brew. It wasn't strong enough to put hair on a man's chest, but it came close. Had to like that.

She gnawed her lip and lifted her chin. "I've been fascinated with Texas since I read about it as a teenager, and this job seemed like the perfect opportunity to fulfill a dream. Brooke interviewed me over the phone and hired me."

"So you decided to pack everything you own in the back of your car and satisfy your curiosity?"

"Yes."

He couldn't imagine loading up his truck and leaving his family behind. This patch of land in McMullen County, Texas, was his home. Two of his brothers had left home, but they'd had good reasons. Brand had traveled the rodeo circuit for ten years because they'd needed his winnings to hold on to the ranch. Cort had gone all the way to North Carolina for college because he'd had a partial scholarship at Duke.

Why had Leanna left home? Uprooting herself for a temporary job didn't make sense. "Are you on the run?"

Her face paled, and her eyes widened. "From what?"

"Or whom."

"I'm not running from anything or anyone." She sounded pretty defensive for somebody who had nothing to hide.

"What did your family say when you took off?"

She glanced away. "I don't have any family who'll worry about me."

He recognized a dodge when he saw one, and something in her tone didn't sound right. "Show me your ID."

"What?" She set her mug down on the counter with a thump.

"You look like a teenager. Your car's packed with God-knows-what. You *allegedly* leave a job in a movie star's mansion to hide out on a dude ranch halfway across the country. It doesn't add up. I figure either you're lying about your age or you're on the run. For all I know you could have robbed the dead guy and skedaddled across the state line."

Folding her arms across her chest, she frowned. "You're incredibly suspicious."

He pulled his gaze away from the taut fabric stretched over her breasts. "Did you steal his silver?"

She gaped at him. *"No."*

"Nothing crammed in your car belonged to Arch Golden?"

Guilty pink climbed her cheeks. "I didn't sneak anything out of Arch's house."

Yep. Evasive. "Where's the ID?"

"I don't have it with me." He made a face and she continued, "I showed all the proper documentation to Brooke yesterday. I didn't bring my purse today."

Right. He'd never known a woman who went anywhere without the arsenal she carried in her purse. "Where is it?"

Again she averted her gaze. "I...I left it under...my bed."

Sure she had. "Lemme see your car's registration."

"My car is at Pete's."

She had an answer for everything, but the last one he could and would check out with a phone call. Brooke had left him in charge, and danged if he'd let anything go wrong. His days of letting folks down were over. "How'd he die?"

She blinked and shook her head as if he'd surprised her. "Who? Arch?"

He nodded.

"Lung cancer. Do you smoke?"

What difference did it make if he did? "Never have. Expensive habit. You?"

"No." She fiddled with the hem of her shirt.

"Do you have any secrets I need to know about, kid?"

Her deer-in-the-headlights expression sent alarm bells clanging in his mind. "Secrets?"

His gut twisted into one big knot of apprehension. Aw hell, Brooke, what have you dumped on me? He didn't have time to police the Double C's hostess. "Vices. Bad habits."

"As many as your average citizen, I guess."

An average citizen from a Hollywood movie star's neighborhood was a whole different species from the folks he was used to dealing with. He couldn't head off a problem if he'd never heard of it. "Like what?"

She rubbed her forehead with one long, slender finger. Her hand was steady and her skin and eyes were clear. He could probably rule out substance abuse.

"I have a weakness for jelly beans."

He snorted in disbelief. "Now that's scary. What else?"

She angled her chin and narrowed her eyes. "I like lobster with drawn butter and two-hour bubble baths."

And just like that, his body took that wrong-way detour again. A picture of Leanna in a tub with her long hair piled on top of her head and bubbles teasing the tops of her breasts immediately formed in his mind. He chugged several sips of coffee to distract himself from that irrational, illogical, *impossible* fantasy and scalded his tongue.

What in the hell was wrong with him that he'd be fantasizing about a gal still wet behind the ears? Wasn't thirty-six too young for a midlife crisis?

She arched a brow. "You?"

"Ask anybody. I have more vices than any man ought to."

She frowned and shoved away from the counter. "If I want to figure out where everything is and go over the menus and cabin assignments before the others arrive I should get started."

She hightailed it out of the room, leaving him wondering what he'd said to make her run away.

Leanna closed a guest room door, moved on to check the towels, sheets and soaps in the next one. She'd give anything to crawl into one of those beds and sleep for a couple of hours.

Darkness had fallen by the time Pete had dropped her off at the dude ranch entrance last night, and after lugging her suitcases up the mile-long driveway, she'd been too tired to poke around in the inky shadows looking for a place to sleep. Since Brooke had mentioned that the ranch would be empty for the night, she'd stashed her luggage under the porch and crashed on a lounge chair. Luckily she'd packed bug repellant because the mosquitoes here were huge, and they liked California cuisine—namely *her*.

At first light she'd found the barn and made use of the big concrete stall used for washing the horses to shower and change clothes. With a little snooping, she'd found an out-of-the-way building which looked to be unused except for furniture storage. After picking the lock, she'd stashed her bags and returned to the main house, only to drift off to sleep while waiting for Patrick to arrive.

She yawned and arched her stiff back. Living with Arch had spoiled her. She used to be able to sleep anywhere. Tonight she looked forward to stretching out on the long sofa in the storage building, without the bugs. Maybe Rico would keep her company. She'd felt safe with the tough-looking dog beside her.

As she moved from room to room, her mind drifted back to this morning's conversation with Patrick. He'd said he and his father didn't get along. That was good—at least as far as the inheritance went. He might be reluctant to announce his true paternity if he and the man who'd raised him were close.

She wondered if Mr. Lander knew Patrick wasn't his son. Carolyn's letters suggested he didn't. If he didn't, her surprise wouldn't be a pleasant one.

After Arch made it in Hollywood, he'd written to Carolyn wanting to claim his son. She'd promised to write again when she'd broken the news to Patrick about his true paternity and asked her husband for a divorce. The letter never came, because Carolyn had died.

Stopping in front of the mirror, she smoothed her

hair and reapplied her tinted lip balm. Her mother constantly urged her to "do something with herself," fearing she'd never catch a man if she continued her plain-Jane ways. Tonya, who'd had more lovers than Tootsie had rolls, couldn't understand that not every woman wanted to depend on a man to keep food on the table and a roof over her head.

The last thing Leanna wanted to do was give someone the power to break her heart. She'd nursed her mother's broken hearts for most of her life and wasn't eager to drag herself through that morass.

She closed the door on the last room and made her way down the wide staircase to the small office. It'd be wise to go over the registration packets for each of their guests so she would know whom she'd be expected to entertain and what kinds of interests the guests might have.

As soon as she entered Brooke and Caleb's private quarters, the smell of fresh paint and the rumble of voices told her the decorators had arrived. She jerked to a halt inside the office.

Patrick sat at the desk with his head bent over a stack of papers. In profile, he looked so much like Arch that her heart ached and her throat clogged with loss. Soon, after they got to know each other a little better, she'd tell him about Arch. The truth would be easier coming from a friend than a stranger.

"Patrick, could I get the keys to the cabins?"

His dark eyes focused on her and the image of her mentor vanished. Arch had been an attractive man, but he hadn't oozed sensuality the way Patrick did. Patrick was the kind of man who made a woman stand up straighter and hold her shoulders back.

"Sure. Need anything else?" Frown lines scored his forehead, as if something were bothering him.

"I'd like to go over the registration packets."

"They're in the basket, but I've already double-checked them. Everything's in 'em." He reached into the drawer and pulled out a key ring with at least three dozen keys on it. "The keys are marked with the cabin numbers."

If one of those went to the storage building, she wouldn't have to pick the lock tonight. Her fingertips brushed his palm when she took the keys. A tingle traveled all the way up her arm. Alarmed, she snatched her hand back. "Thank you."

"You can meet the crew after lunch." He drummed his fingers on the desk.

"Fine. I'll go check the cabins." She'd look over the packets later. The office was too small for both of them to work in without tripping over each other, and his blatant masculinity was...overpowering. She turned to leave.

"Leanna, how old was Arch Golden?" His question stopped her at the door.

She turned and could have sworn his eyes were focused on her bottom before he blinked and met her gaze. A flush spread from her middle through her limbs. "Fifty-nine. Why?"

"He was too old for you."

Her shoulders sagged. Patrick wasn't the first to jump to the wrong conclusion about her relationship with Arch. "Arch wasn't my lover."

He sat back in the chair, lacing his fingers over his flat belly and stretching his long legs out in front of him. "Then what was he?"

"A friend." A mentor, a father figure, a safe harbor.

He'd given her a home when she'd felt unsafe in her own.

"Right." There was that sarcasm again. "You lived with him almost six years."

Seven if you counted the year he and her mother had been a couple, but that wasn't common knowledge. Arch had done his best to shield her from the press. "How do you know that?"

Muttering under his breath, he swiveled back to the desk.

"You know, Patrick, every relationship between a man and a woman doesn't have to be sexual."

His scowl bordered on ferocious. "A relationship between a man and a child sure as hell shouldn't be— unless he's a pervert."

"Your—Arch was not a pervert. He was a kind and generous and…" But Patrick wasn't listening. He'd focused his attention on the papers in front of him. Her name nearly leaped off the page. She moved closer. "What are you reading?"

"The report on you."

"What?" She halted midstep.

"Brooke orders background checks on every employee—including you. Although yours is sketchy because it was done on short notice."

Anger rippled through her like waves on a pond. He had some nerve going through her confidential files. She reached for it, but he pulled it out of reach. "That's private information. You have no right—"

"I have every right to know what kind of employee I'm responsible for supervising."

Maybe he did, but she didn't want her dirty laundry aired. She snatched at the report again. He put a hand out to hold her back. His fingers splayed over her waist, distracting her from her goal. Alarmed by the unexpected contact and even more by the heat pooling beneath his fingers, she jumped back.

He fisted his hand in his lap. "You said you had no family. Does your sister know where you are?"

She winced at the hurt his words inflicted and sank back on her heels. One of these days she'd get used to Tonya's lies. "I don't have a sister."

He tapped the page on the desk in front of him as if seeing it in print made it a fact.

She huffed out an exasperated breath. "You need a better investigator. The woman who claims to be my sister is actually my mother. She lies about her age to get parts."

"She's an actress?" He obviously wasn't a Hollywood fan.

"Not one you've ever heard of. And in case your lousy snoop missed it, *she* was Arch's lover, not me." She turned to leave once again.

"Is Golden your father?"

Leanna bit her tongue to keep from yelling, *No, he's yours.* Patrick had no idea how lucky he was to have not one, but two men who wanted to claim him. If that wasn't enough, according to Carolyn's letters, he'd been his mother's favorite son as well.

She had no one except a mother who'd only become interested in her when a millionaire had taken her under his wing. Her own father had been horrified when she'd looked him up and introduced herself. He'd threatened to call the police if she didn't leave him alone.

"Arch didn't come into our lives until I was twelve. My mother didn't tell me who my father was until I turned eighteen, and she only told me then because I threatened to hire one of those agencies to find him."

She hated revealing her dirty secret, but he'd find out sooner or later, and she hoped he wouldn't hold her mongrel background against her.

"We lived with Arch for about a year and then moved on. I returned later—without my mother."

He closed his eyes and pinched the bridge of his nose. "Hell, I'm sorry."

"Save your pity. You can't miss what you never had." But she did. More than anything, she wanted to be part of a strong family unit. For a while Arch had been that for her. But now he was gone, and with each hour that passed, it looked less and less like Patrick would fill his father's shoes.

Three

The way the dude ranch crew tumbled into the kitchen reminded Leanna of a litter of eager puppies.

The staff came in all shapes and sizes, more males than females, but their camaraderie made it clear that they were all glad to be here.

A man about Patrick's age straddled a chair and called out, "Wanna know what the bet's up to now, Romeo? One month. My fifty bucks says you can't make it."

Leanna glanced at Patrick, hoping he'd enlighten her, but he flushed and avoided her gaze. "You're full of it, Toby."

"Won't be me full of rising sap."

"*My* money says he won't make it past Saturday night," another man called out.

One of the women shushed them. "Leave him alone."

Curiosity and her own competitive nature got the better of Leanna. "What's the bet?"

"We're betting—"

Patrick interrupted Toby. "Folks, this is Leanna. She's filling in for Brooke. Introduce yourselves."

But Toby wasn't dissuaded. He continued, "I'm Toby, trail boss, and I'm betting Patrick can't stay away from Red Dog's Bar or women until Caleb gets back."

Leanna chewed the inside of her cheek. Womanizing and drinking. That didn't sound good. Was Patrick a loser like her mother's exes? She hoped not.

The group doled out names and job descriptions until only one man, about her age, was left. He ambled toward her and didn't stop until he'd crowded her against the counter. "Sweet thing, I'd love to show you the local sights."

Leanna's heart raced and her muscles constricted. The last man who'd called her "sweet thing" had tried to rape her. The counter pressed into her spine, reminding her too much of the slick shower stall. Cold sweat beaded her lip, but she stood her ground. "No, thanks. I bought a map."

"A map can't show you half what—"

"I prefer fact to fiction, and I suspect you're full of it."

She heard snickers from the crew.

"Back off, Warren." Patrick clamped a hand on the man's shoulder and yanked him out of her space. "She said no."

Patrick turned, putting his broad shoulders between her and the rest of the crew. Leanna fought the nausea stirring her stomach and tried to steady her nerves as Patrick gave orders for the day.

The encounter had surprised her. Flirtatious creeps had been a part of her life for as long as she could remember. Usually she could spot them a mile off and defend herself from them, but she'd let down her guard in the crowded kitchen.

The crew emptied out of the kitchen, and Patrick turned to face her. "Are you all right?"

"Fine." She tried to smile, but her lips quivered.

"Right. That's why you look like you're gonna toss your cookies on my boots."

The concern in his eyes wrapped around her like a warm blanket. No one besides Arch had ever stood up for her before. "Your imagination is working overtime."

"Is there something you're not telling me, kid?"

If only he knew. "Stop calling me kid."

"I'll stop when you tell me what you're really doing here." He continued to study her until she wanted to squirm. She wouldn't tell him the truth until he knew her well enough to trust her when she told him how much Arch had cared about him.

She held his gaze, trying to act as if she hadn't nearly had a panic attack. The concern on Patrick's face slowly changed. His features tightened. His gaze heated and dropped to her mouth.

Her nerves clamored again, but panic wasn't the cause. An unknown emotion spread through her, shortening her breath and making her skin prickle.

Patrick shook his head and took a step back. He turned on his heel and called over his shoulder, "Ring the brass bell on the back porch if you need me."

The sun was a dim light on the horizon when Patrick parked his truck beside the barn. The sound of running

water had him swearing and jogging toward the washing stall, but it wasn't a busted pipe that made his knees
lock up and his jaw drop.

Leanna was naked.

She had her back to him as she rinsed the shampoo
from her hair with the nozzle she held in one hand.
Water and bubbles slid from her shoulders to the nip
of her waist, faithfully following her curves the way a
skilled lover would with his hands. Suds washed over
the bow of her hips, her taut pale behind, and down
long, sleek legs to puddle around her shower sandals
before swirling down the drain.

His throat knotted up and his heart hammered. His
blood headed south. He was rock-hard in an instant.

He ought to let her know he was here. Better yet, he
should get outta here. His feet wouldn't move, but his
eyes sure did, savoring the feast of a beautiful, wet
woman.

Get a grip, Lander. You've seen naked ladies before.
Dozens of them. But why in the hell was *this one*
showering in the barn? He couldn't ask. His mouth was
as dry as dirt.

Slowly she rotated, but her eyes remained closed.
Full, pale breasts with tightly puckered dusky tips. A
tiny waist. Rounded hips. A tangle of dark curls framed
by a narrow triangle of lighter skin.

Leanna was built better than any wet dream he'd
ever had. Air gushed from his lungs.

Her lids flew open. The shock in her eyes gave way
to fear—the same fear he'd seen in her eyes yesterday
when Warren had hit on her. She reached for the knob
behind her and turned off the hot water, and then aimed
the hose right at his crotch. "Cool off, cowboy."

A blast of frigid water jerked him out of his trance.

She redirected the spray to his face, knocking off his hat and soaking him from head to toe. "Hey!"

Bounding forward, he grabbed the hose. Leanna wrestled him for it. His knuckles brushed her silky belly. Her breast hit his biceps like an electric cattle prod.

She gasped and jerked back, tripping over the hose coiled at her feet. Her arms flailed.

He tried to catch her and keep her from falling on the concrete, but his hands slipped on the slick, wet skin of her back. Before he knew it he had a handful of her soft bottom, and her pebbled nipples branded a hole through his wet shirt.

Every cell in his body rose for "Reveille."

"Cut it out." He said it to himself as much as to her. She stopped struggling, but remained rigid in his arms. He righted her, released her and turned off the water, even though he seriously needed to aim the icy flow down the front of his Wranglers.

Covering her breasts and the curls between her legs with her hands, she backed as far away from him as she could in the confines of the wash stall.

Although he would have preferred to make another leisurely inspection of her figure, the wariness in her eyes stopped him cold. He snatched the towel hanging from the hook on the wall beside him and tossed it to her.

She caught it and swiftly wound it around herself, but she didn't take her gaze off him—not even long enough to blink.

He had to say something. While he'd never had trouble talking to a naked woman before, he didn't have a clue what to say now. Might as well start with the obvious. "Why are you showering in the barn at four-thirty in the morning?"

"Y-you're early."

"Last I heard, the Pink Palace had running water."

"I'm…I'm not st-staying at the rooming house."

"Why?"

Her brows dipped and she chewed her bottom lip. "I can't afford it."

He shoved the wet hair off his forehead and swiped the water from his face. "Why in the hell didn't you say so?"

She tipped up her chin and squared her shoulders, but her white-knuckled grip on the towel didn't loosen. "I would have been fine if you hadn't come early."

Fine if he hadn't… He rubbed the back of his neck. How did this get to be *his* fault? "Where did you sleep last night?"

She pressed her lips together and remained mute.

"Tell me or you're fired."

She opened her mouth and closed it again.

Water trickled off his wet clothes, filling his favorite boots. He was beginning to suspect he'd be looking for a new hostess when she said, "In one of the storage buildings."

"One of the—" He snapped his jaw shut on the stampede of curses battling to get out.

"I'm used to making do. It's fine."

Fury built in him. He wanted to hit something. Or someone. Snatching up his soggy hat, he dusted it off on his pants leg and rammed it back on his head. The background check hadn't mentioned any man in Leanna's past other than Arch Golden. That bastard must be responsible for the fear darkening her eyes and making her tremble.

She looked like she expected him to pounce on her any second. If Golden weren't already dead he'd like to teach the SOB a lesson in manners—with his fists.

"You have ten minutes to get dressed, collect your gear and haul your butt to my truck."

"Why?" Suspicion clouded her eyes.

"Because I'm taking you home. You're staying at Crooked Creek until a room opens up at the Double C."

She tipped up her chin. "What if I don't want to?"

"Then you're fired." He headed out the door.

"I...I..." Her sputtering made him turn back.

"Your choice. My truck or the highway. You have nine minutes left." He turned and sloshed out of the barn.

When he reached his truck he sat on the open tailgate, yanked off his first boot, emptied the water from it and flung it into the truck bed. It hit the bedliner with a satisfying *thunk*.

Dammit. He'd been around more than his share of women, but he'd never given a single one of them reason to fear him. Hell, it didn't matter that he'd been stiffer than a fence post when he held Leanna. He'd never force a woman.

He rolled off his soggy sock, sent it the way of the boot and tugged off the second boot and sock.

Her fear both yesterday and today knotted his stomach. What had happened to Leanna? And why in the hell did it anger him to the point of violence? The urge to protect her was unexpected. No one, other than his family, had ever drawn such a visceral reaction from him.

He looked up and spotted her walking toward him with a smooth, hip-rolling, pulse-accelerating gate. She wore her checkered dude ranch uniform shirt over a pair of snug jeans. What that woman did to good ol' denim ought to be outlawed. She definitely warranted a wanted poster, because every man who spotted her would want to get her alone in the hayloft. Including him.

No, not him, he corrected. Off-limits, Lander. He didn't have time to dally with any woman right now. Easing a skittish one was out of the question. And unless he was mistaken, Leanna was afraid of men. The ache in his groin guaranteed he was definitely male.

She stopped in front of him. "I'm not staying at your place unless you let me pay my way."

"I thought you were broke."

She wet her lips and tucked a damp strand of hair behind her ear. "I can pay in other ways."

His libido kicked into high gear despite a serious attempt to rein it in. He cast his gaze skyward, wondering what he'd done to deserve such torture. It had to be that temporary vow of celibacy. *Somebody*—he glared at the biggest cloud—seemed determined to test him by sending an inexperienced gal his way—one who needed protecting from wolves like him. One who had no business showing up in his dreams like she had last night.

He probably didn't want to know the answer, but he had to ask. "What did you have in mind?"

"I'll cook and clean for you around my work schedule here."

It wasn't the offer he'd expected, but he wasn't disappointed. *He wasn't.* Hell, she was a decade too young for him, and he'd vowed to behave himself until Caleb returned. He would not be tempted.

Scratch that. He wouldn't give in to temptation.

Somebody had hurt Leanna in the past. The last thing he wanted to do was hurt her again, and with his relationship track record, hurt was about the only thing he could guarantee.

He opened his mouth to refuse her offer, but he reconsidered when she stiffened her shoulders. He had a feeling she'd walk if he refused. The dudes were due in a few hours. Even if he wanted to boot her out— and he was beginning to suspect he didn't—he'd never find another hostess in time.

"Deal. Get in."

Patrick's house looked like something from the pages of Leanna's favorite Americana calendar—the one she stared at when she dreamed of owning her own place.

All it lacked were hanging baskets of colorful flowers to make it perfect. If this were her home she'd trim the untamed daisies flanking the front steps of the white two-story structure and put the blooms in a vase on the kitchen table. Each evening she'd watch the sun set from one of the oversize rocking chairs lining the railing of the porch.

She followed Patrick across the plank floor. All she had to do was get her mother straightened out, finish college, and land a good-paying job, then she could start saving for a home.

Patrick glanced at her, and her cheeks flushed with embarrassment for the way she'd overreacted earlier. He didn't know she had good reason to be wary of men who sneaked up on her when she showered. He probably just thought she was nuts.

When she'd first turned around, her vision had been obscured by shampoo and water. By the time she'd recognized Patrick they'd been chest to chest, her legs tangled with his, his belt buckle pressing into her belly.

His very obvious arousal had startled her. Worse, it had stirred something deep inside her that she didn't want to analyze too closely. His touch had been helpful rather than hurtful, but she hadn't been able to erase the bad memories and she'd panicked.

And now he was carrying her home like a stray kitten. Like father, like son. Arch had done the same when he'd found her. It seemed both men had a penchant for collecting strays.

"Don't bring your women here, boy."

She jerked her gaze to the older man sitting at the kitchen table. He eyed her as if she was something the cat had dragged in and then scowled at Patrick. "You're wet."

Patrick closed the door behind her. "Unexpected shower. Leanna's not one of my women, Pop. She's Brooke's stand-in, and she needs a place to stay. Leanna Jensen. Jack Lander."

Her breath caught, and she swallowed hard. This man thought he was Patrick's father. He was the one most likely to be hurt by her revelation. How would he handle the news? Her conscience prickled. "Hello."

An almost imperceptible nod was her only response. "Where you puttin' her?"

"In Caleb's room." Patrick padded barefoot across the kitchen and headed up the stairs with her suitcases.

She paused, uncertain whether to follow Patrick or…

Jack took the decision out of her hands. "Go on. Git. You two got enough to do today without standing around making small talk. Tell him I'll handle those college boys so he doesn't have to come back again."

"Thank you for letting me stay. I'll get out of your

way as soon as I get my first paycheck. I've promised Patrick I'd cook and clean to pay my way.''

''Sounds fair. We get by, but I'm danged sick of my own cooking. His, too. Never did like to push a broom.'' He put on his hat and headed for the door.

Jack Lander was nice. It made her feel ten times worse for the bomb she'd soon drop on his life. ''Mr. Lander, it's supposed to be over a hundred degrees today. You might want to carry a water bottle or something.''

He scowled at her, but the venom in his expression didn't reach his eyes. ''Don't coddle me, girl. I'm too old for it.''

His gruff attitude reminded her so much of Arch that her heart ached and her eyes stung. ''I don't think any of us ever get too old for someone to care.''

He crossed to the sink and filled a thermos with water. After he let himself out the back door she reluctantly climbed the steps. Through the open doors off the hall she could see four bedrooms—two on each end of the landing. Patrick exited one, peeling his wet shirt from his body.

Darkly tanned skin wrapped the well-defined muscles of his chest and shoulders. A triangle of hair dusted the space between his flat nipples and trailed down over his firm, ridged belly to the waist of his wet jeans.

She'd seen her share of beautiful bodies beside Arch's pool. She'd even dated a few of Arch's guests, but none had sent the ripple of awareness fluttering through her midsection the way Patrick did. It was a scary, out-of-control feeling—probably the same one that had led her mother on many a wild-goose chase.

She took an involuntary step back and nearly fell down the stairs.

Lightning fast, Patrick grabbed her upper arms and hauled her forward. The sheer strength of his grasp sent her stumbling against him. His hot bare skin seared her through the thin fabric of her shirt, and her senses rioted. Alarmed, she put her palms on his shoulders and pushed.

Patrick immediately released her. His features tightened. "On a ranch it pays to watch your step. I have to change. Your stuff's in there." He jerked a thumb toward the room he'd vacated. "No time to unpack. Get what you need for today and we'll go." He disappeared into the next room.

Leanna pressed a hand over her racing heart. Twice now she'd been in Patrick's arms and he hadn't taken advantage. Not even when she'd been naked. Was he the gentleman his mother had described so eloquently? Or was he a womanizing charmer? One was her dream guy, the other a reminder of her mother's many failed attempts to find love.

She made her way inside the room. Her suitcases lay on the wide bed. Through an open door she spotted a connecting bathroom and caught a glimpse of Patrick's room on the opposite side before he closed his door. Her gaze dropped to the door knob and some of her tension drained. The lock was the sturdy old-fashioned kind that was difficult to pick.

If Patrick was the gentleman his mother described in her letters, there wouldn't be any problems. But she had her doubts. Out of the legion of men her mother had paraded through their lives, none had possessed the qualities Carolyn Lander described. Only Arch had come close.

She stepped into the bathroom to reapply her tinted lip balm and grimaced at herself in the mirror. *Advertise your assets.* She could almost hear her mother's chastising voice, but deep inside, Leanna would never be comfortable drawing attention to herself.

Arch had always claimed she was a throwback to the days when actresses had curves instead of eating disorders. All she knew was that her shape had brought her unwanted attention since puberty. She'd learned to draw as little attention to herself as possible and to find out-of-the-way places to play.

She'd been exploring Arch's attic when she'd discovered the cedar cigar humidor holding Carolyn Lander's letters. For the remaining months her mother and Arch had been a couple, she'd spent countless hours reading and rereading the stories of the young cowboy. The humidor had been the first thing she'd searched for when she'd moved back in with Arch years later.

And now she'd met the cowboy face-to-face.

She returned to her room. Patrick, in dry jeans, another checked shirt, and a pair of dry boots leaned against her doorjamb. "Ready?"

"Yes." Her stomach did that fluttery thing. She laid a hand over it and prayed this wasn't a sign that she'd inherited her mother's weakness for falling in and out of love and consequently, in and out of rehab.

"Then, let's go. I'm an hour behind and I haven't even had breakfast."

"That's not my fault. If you hadn't interrupted my shower and insisted on bringing me here, you wouldn't be late."

Shaking his head, he turned and headed down the stairs. "Female logic is the damnedest thing. I guess it's my fault you drove all the way to Texas from California and fried your transmission too?''

She followed him. ''You called Pete and checked my story.''

''Right.''

''Don't you trust anyone?''

Patrick stopped abruptly on the bottom step and turned. ''Been lied to a few times too many.''

And here she was misleading him again. She hoped he'd forgive her. ''Jack asked me to tell you that he'd take care of the college boys—whatever that means.''

They stood eye-to-eye, close enough for her to see the tension drain from his face. Close enough to see the fine lines around his eyes. Close enough to taste his minty breath on her lips. Her pulse accelerated.

''It means he's not going to be pigheaded. *Today.*'' He turned around and headed out the way they'd come in.

She jogged after him. ''Is he usually?''

He held open the door for her to pass through. ''Oh, yeah.''

''About what?'' She followed him to the truck. He opened the door and waited for her to climb into the cab. Gallant. She smiled to herself. Some of the traits Carolyn had attributed to her son were still there.

''His health, mainly.''

''Is he ill?'' Mr. Lander shared the same tired pallor Arch had in his last year.

He didn't answer until he was behind the wheel and buckled in. ''He says he's not.''

The tightness of his voice told her he didn't agree. ''Have you taken him to the doctor?''

''Be easier to shave a barn cat.''

Her brows hiked up in surprise. "Would you do that?"

He flashed his lady-killer grin and her heart stuttered. Patrick Lander was definitely a charmer. Obviously, she'd learned nothing from the soap opera of her mother's life, because the quickening of her heart meant she was attracted to him. She'd promised herself to reserve her heart for a hero.

"Not unless you want to be mauled. Hold on tight. We're taking a shortcut."

He swung the truck onto a rutted track. The first bump jarred her out of her seat and almost into his lap. Her hand brushed his thigh. She scrambled back to her side of the bench seat, fastened her seat belt and clenched her fists.

"Why doesn't your father retire?"

"This ranch is his life. The day he quits working will be the day they tie a toe tag on him."

Carolyn had said much the same thing in her letters. She'd claimed Jack loved the land more than anything or anyone—including her. Evidently, that hadn't changed in the past twenty years.

"And then what will you do?"

He shrugged and downshifted to climb out of the dry creek bed. "Keep ranching, I guess."

His voice lacked the enthusiasm she'd expected. Didn't he have a burning desire to live on the land of his ancestors like Jack? Or was he like so many of the actors she'd met who couldn't wait to leave their small hometowns to make it big somewhere else? "There can't be much money in ranching. The TV news says beef prices are down."

"We'll never be rich, but we've earned what we have."

Her stomach knotted. "You wouldn't want to win the lottery or...inherit a few million dollars?"

"There's no challenge in taking handouts." His eyes scanned the fields as they passed. Who knew what he was looking for? All she saw were grass and black cattle. His dark gaze swung her way.

"Today we start with lunch for the staff and the guests at the welcome barbecue. We'll show folks around the common areas, check 'em in, and give 'em an overview of what to expect for the next five days. Tonight we'll have a local band and a bigger cookout. Don't get caught up in dancing and forget to eat."

"Dancing?"

"Yep. If a guest needs a partner you volunteer. Nobody stands on the sidelines. This week is all about showing folks a good time." His gaze raked over her, and her skin tingled as if he'd touched her. "Within reason. Don't go off alone with anybody. We don't do background checks on the guests. Never know who might turn up."

"I'm sure I won't have any problems."

He shook his head and stared out the windshield. The muscles in his jaw clenched and his hands tightened on the steering wheel. "Leanna, you're a cute kid. Sometimes that's all it takes to cause trouble."

Sometimes, she'd learned, trouble didn't wait for a cause.

Four

The dude ranch welcome reception was like every birthday party she'd never had.

After a cutthroat game of volleyball and another of horseshoes, Leanna had dragged out her slingshot for a less vigorous activity. For the last hour the teens had taken turns shooting at tin cans, but she'd sent them off for refreshments. Now the area was blissfully quiet.

Grinning, she leaned against a hay bale. This was fun.

"Cool off, cowgirl," Patrick said from behind her.

She spun around to find him holding tall glasses of lemonade. Her cheeks heated at the reminder of this morning's embarrassing encounter.

Was he a charmer or charming host? For the last hour she'd watched him flirt with every female from toddler to retiree. On the other hand, if one of the women took him too seriously, he backed off, drew the line and made it very clear he wasn't crossing it. Did that make him a tease or just someone who knew how to ensure the guests had a good time?

She took the glass he offered. "Thanks."

"Where'd you learn to shoot a slingshot?"

She nearly choked on the tart drink. "I-it's a hobby I picked up as a teen."

As soon as she'd read in Carolyn's letters that Patrick was a whiz with a slingshot she'd been determined to learn. She fingered the knotty handle of the one she'd made from a Y-shaped branch and rubber bands when her mother refused to buy one. Even though she'd later earned enough money to afford one, her homemade version remained her favorite, because it was a project she and Arch had done together. In the last year when Arch had had little energy for anything else, they'd shot target practice in his garden.

"Good idea." He nodded to the line of empty soda cans she'd set up along the top of the fence. "I used to be pretty good with one of those."

She offered him her slingshot and a cup of rocks. "Give it a try."

He looked tempted but hesitant. "It's been a while."

"Afraid I'll outshoot you? I am good."

A competitive light fired his eyes. "Kid, I might be rusty, but shooting isn't something you forget."

"I'll allow you a few practice shots. I won't even watch in case you embarrass yourself." She grinned at his stunned expression and turned her back. A few seconds later she heard the whiz of the rock. She counted five shots before another whiz followed by a ping told her he'd connected with his target. She waited while he took a few more shots and then faced him again.

"Ready?" When he nodded she jogged to the fence and reset the cans.

He offered her the slingshot and she declined with a shake of her head. "You're on a roll. Don't stop now."

He knocked down seven of the ten cans, handed her the slingshot and crossed the yard to reset the targets. He ambled back to her side, tucked his thumbs into his pockets and rocked back on his heels. The cocky challenge in his eyes was unmistakable. "Let's see if you can back up all that braggin'."

She could. Without kids her own age to play with, she'd had hours to practice. Taking the overconfident cowboy down a peg would be pure pleasure. "Are you willing to place a wager?"

He pursed his lips. "What'd you have in mind?"

If she wanted to earn his friendship and his trust she had to find ways to spend time with him. "If I win, then you have to take me to the Pink Palace on my first day off. I want to see the haunted room."

His brows dipped. "The ghost only comes out when the couple's…amorous."

Her heart slammed against her ribs, and her palms moistened. Surely she could handle a simple kiss? She'd been kissed before. "Do you think a kiss would be amorous enough?"

His mental step back was as clear as the Waterford crystal he'd inherit from Arch. "Leanna—"

His lack of interest in her in that way both soothed and annoyed her. "I'll hold your hand so you won't be scared."

He stiffened his spine and set his mouth in a determined line. "You're on. One kiss. No tongues."

Her heart stuttered and her cheeks burned at the thought of kissing him that intimately. "And if you win?'' He wouldn't, but she might as well make it a fair wager.

''You tell me the real reason you're here.''

She'd have to tell him soon, anyway. ''Deal.''

She took down the first six cans with ease, but then he leaned against the hay bale, crowding into her space. His scent teased and distracted her. She missed the next two cans. Adjusting her grip on the handle, she tried to regain her focus.

''Lose your nerve?'' he taunted in a low rumbling voice that sent a shiver of awareness down her spine.

The taunting slant of his smile raised her competitive hackles. She took down the last two cans and grinned at him even though her stomach felt as if she'd swallowed a school of goldfish. Patrick would be kissing her. ''You owe me.''

''Right.'' He didn't look overjoyed.

The teens returned. Leanna passed the slingshot to one of the girls. ''Back to work for me.''

Patrick hesitated. ''What I came to say was thanks for handling that kid earlier. I was ready to toss him into the pool if he asked me one more time why the ranch didn't have Nintendo. Can't say I'd have ever thought of a watermelon-seed-spitting contest.''

He should have. According to Carolyn, he'd been the champion seed-spitter in his family.

''You don't like children?'' His mother's letters said that Patrick always volunteered to watch his younger siblings.

He shrugged. ''I don't have much experience with them, but I know I'm not crazy about the whiny ones.''

She bit her lip and wondered how she could quiz him without revealing knowledge she shouldn't have.

"Didn't you get stuck baby-sitting your younger brothers? Older siblings usually do."

"That was more than twenty years ago and *stuck* is the right word. I wanted to work with my father, but he always took Caleb along and left me at the house."

Had she misunderstood Carolyn's letters? Impossible, considering how many times she'd read them.

Leanna's musical laugh drew Patrick's attention across the crowd gathered on the lantern-lit patio.

Her gaze met his and a slow smile curved her lips. Danged if his blood didn't heat just like it had every other time their eyes had met tonight. She said goodbye to her dance partner and headed in his direction.

Oh, hell.

He'd looked up a dozen times tonight and caught her watching him. She'd flash him a shy smile and go back to working her way through the crowd, pairing up folks with similar interests. For the life of him he couldn't figure out why she'd singled him out when there were plenty of willing fellas closer to her age. All of the teenage boys were panting over her. But she watched him.

He'd have to set her straight before he did something stupid. Like respond. It was becoming damned near impossible to resist that grin of hers.

She sidled up to him with that mind-bending walk of hers. "Dance with me, Patrick?"

No way. "Leanna—"

"You said I should drag anyone standing on the sidelines out onto the floor and into the action."

He grimaced. Yeah, he'd said that.

"You're the only laggard." The sweep of her hand indicated the guests, and sure enough, everyone else was involved in one activity or another. Even the kids were occupied.

But dancing with her wasn't a risk he was willing to take. He looked around for an escape and cursed silently when he didn't find one. If his buddies could see him now, running from a gal still wet behind the ears, he'd never live it down. *Running,* for crying out loud. Patrick Lander never ran from women. More often than not he accepted the invitations to dance—vertically or horizontally—without thinking twice. But not this time. Not with a gal who kept inviting him to play when he was trying to be serious. "I'm working here."

"Afraid you can't keep up with me?"

The dare in her eyes stirred his competitive blood. His common sense reminded him of the butt-kicking he'd taken from her dare this afternoon. But common sense didn't keep his mouth shut.

"Sweetheart, the question isn't whether or not *I* could keep up with *you.* It's whether or not I'd leave you eating my dust. I am good." He winked and threw her earlier words back at her.

Leanna grinned and offered her hand. He ought to be ashamed of himself for letting an amateur angler hook him. Patrick let her reel him onto the floor. The least he could do was make her defeat quick and painless.

For three dances he spun, dipped and twirled her, using every intricate dance move he knew—and he knew 'em all. Leanna never missed a step. It'd been ages since he'd had a partner who could keep up with him, and he'd forgotten how much he loved dancing. More than once he caught himself grinning right back at her.

The band finished the last song and the guests applauded. He realized they were applauding him and Leanna as much as the band. He hadn't noticed the floor had cleared, because he'd been too focused on his partner—on the brush of their bodies and on the victorious sweep of her gold-tipped lashes each time he tried and failed to lose her with a complicated step.

Breathless and laughing, she looked up at him. The flush on her cheeks could have been from the attention or from the workout he'd given her. Whatever the cause, she looked damned tempting.

His breathing became unsteady and he felt a little feverish. He had a serious hankering to kiss that sassy smirk right off her lips. He tightened his hands on the smooth muscles of her upper arms and inched her forward.

A wolf whistle brought him back to his right mind. He released her and stepped back.

She arched her brows, and mischief sparkled in her eyes. "Did I forget to mention Arch's last lover was a dance instructor?"

He'd been hustled *twice* by a wet-behind-the-ears gal. Served him right for thinking he was such hot stuff. "It wasn't on your job application."

Shaking his head at his own conceit, he led Leanna off the floor and poured them each a glass of lemonade.

He'd underestimated her abilities as a hostess and a dance partner, and he had to wonder if she had any more surprises in store for him.

More than anything, he wanted to forget that he'd promised to kiss her on Thursday, because damned if he wasn't starting to like the gal more than he should.

Determined to begin earning her keep, Leanna rolled out of bed before sunup and made her way downstairs.

She set the bacon sizzling in the cast iron skillet and mixed a batch of pancake batter. A step creaked and she turned. Patrick descended the stairs carrying his boots in one hand. His unbuttoned shirt flapped against his bare, flat belly.

She nearly dropped an eggshell into the batter.

The man exuded more sex appeal than any movie star she'd ever met—doubly so because his was genuine and not turned on and off like a stage light.

He stopped on the bottom step, looking a little surprised to find the kitchen already occupied. "You're making me look bad, kid."

Impossible. He hadn't shaved and his hair looked as if he'd only taken the time to finger comb it. He must have just tumbled from his bed and poured himself into those snug, low-riding jeans. His raw masculinity overwhelmed her.

She turned back to the stove and briskly whipped the mixture. Her hands shook when she poured the first puddle of batter into the hot pan. In her experience, handsome and charming added up to heartbreak.

"If you want to lie in bed half the day, that's not my problem."

"If I dally in bed it's because somebody's keeping me there. You should try it sometime—with someone your own age."

Her cheeks burned. She'd bet a flock of women vied for that position. "Until I can find a guy whose integrity doesn't vanish in the morning light, I think I'll pass."

"Morning afters can be ugly, that's for sure." He started tucking in his shirttails. It seemed an incredibly intimate thing to witness and made her feel…unsettled.

"I'm going to feed the animals in the barn."

She turned back to the stove. "I'll have breakfast ready by the time you get back."

"Do I smell pancakes?"

He stood directly behind her, looking over her shoulder. His minty breath stirred the hairs on her nape. A shiver worked its way down her spine. "Yes."

"My favorite."

"I—" She bit her tongue before she revealed that she already knew that. "I'm glad you like them."

He snatched a piece of bacon from the platter and sat down at the kitchen table to tug on his boots. "The crew and I'll lead most of the dudes out on a trail ride this morning, but a few stragglers always stay behind. If you're in one of the rooms or cabins and a guest returns, leave."

"I can handle—"

He held up a hand to cut off her words. "That's the rule."

He paused with one hand on the back doorknob. "Be ready to go in thirty minutes."

She'd just added the last of the pancakes to the platter when Jack Lander came downstairs.

"Morning," he grumbled, and shuffled toward the coffeepot.

"Good morning."

"Haven't had a woman cooking in this kitchen in years."

Making friends with Jack and then hurting him seemed underhanded and devious. She passed him a plate and looked for an excuse to get out of the kitchen.

"M'wife used to make pancakes every morning. City gal, like you."

She knew. Arch had called Carolyn the orchid he'd found blooming in a cow pasture. "I should, um...run upstairs and do a little cleaning before heading to the dude ranch.''

She dashed up the steps and paused in the hallway. Given the way his presence seemed to affect her it was best to deal with Patrick's domain while he was absent.

Stepping inside his room felt like an invasion of privacy. Although her room was decorated in a similar style, with sturdy, no-nonsense pine furniture and a wide bed covering most of the hardwood floor, this room smelled of cedar and citrus *and Patrick*. She didn't like the peculiar way her stomach felt.

A row of framed pictures lined the top of his long dresser. A dozen more had been tucked into the frame around the mirror. Curious and more than a little envious because there hadn't been any snapshots from her childhood, she leaned closer to study the dark-haired, dark-eyed men.

She recognized Jack and Caleb, and guessed that the other two men were the younger Lander boys Carolyn had written about. One man held a bull-riding trophy. The other wore a college graduate's cap and gown. All were handsome with similar coloring, but Patrick's features were more classically sculpted, his body a little leaner, and his hair a darker brown.

Patrick's family. Would they be bothered by the revelation that Patrick was only their half brother? Surely not. They'd had a lifetime together.

She turned her back on the photos and tackled the bed, straightening the tangled sheets and yanking up the covers. Footsteps ascended the stairs. She quickly tucked the pillow into place and smoothed the wrinkled case. Turning, she glanced over her shoulder, expecting to see Jack in the hall.

Patrick stepped into the room. ''Leanna, if you're

going to play with a man's sheets you ought to wait until he's with you.''

For the life of her, she couldn't seem to think of a single thing to say. The teasing glint in his eyes made her long for a witty comeback. No such luck. ''I'll…get out of your way.''

He reached for the buttons of his shirt, and she nearly swallowed her tongue. Obviously, undressing in front of women was not an issue for him. ''Give me time to shower and shave and we'll head out.''

The racing of her heart wasn't caused by panic. Surprise glued her feet to the floor.

''You joining me, kid? 'Cause I gotta warn you, it'd be a rush job. And I do hate rushing.'' His voice dropped to a purr for the last line.

His naughty smile and the teasing glint in his eyes made her head spin. She grappled for sanity.

''Save your charm for the dudes, cowboy. I'm not going to fall all over you.'' She ducked around the bed, heading for the exit.

Patrick blocked her path. ''Don't tell me you don't like flirting. You had every guy at the welcome party working up a sweat to get your attention.''

''I'm surprised you could see that over the women piled at your feet.''

''You sound jealous.''

Was she? Certainly not. ''Get your hearing checked.''

He chuckled. ''Do you have a comeback for everything?''

''Usually. Is that a problem?''

''Nah. I like it.'' He reached for his belt buckle, and her eyes nearly bugged out of her head. Was he planning to strip right in front of her? ''Hustle on out of here unless you plan on washing my back. We're late again."

She bolted to her room and pressed her cold hands to her hot cheeks. The splash of the shower sent her mind scurrying down an unwelcome path. On the other side of that door Patrick was peeling down to his bare, tanned skin. Heat pooled in her midsection.

In the past she'd always ended any relationship before it could drift into dangerous waters. This time, running wasn't an option. She had an obligation to Arch to stay and see this through.

Patrick figured it was a good thing he had a way with the little cowpokes. Otherwise he'd have run out of patience about five minutes ago and started banging his head on the corral in frustration.

His first chore on Sunday mornings was to assign a horse to each guest. Usually it wasn't a challenge, but today, one ornery little buckaroo was determined to have the only horse on the property more hardheaded than the kid himself.

"Tim, you'll be responsible for your horse the entire week. Diablo's spoiled rotten. Trust me—he's not the one you want." The thought of Tim cleaning Diablo's hooves made Patrick break out in a cold sweat.

"Is, too." The kid's lip poked out and quivered.

Patrick gritted his teeth and tried to think of a way to say no that an eight-year-old would accept without bawling.

The boy stomped his pint-size feet and screwed up his face. "I want this one."

"That one looks cranky, Tim."

Patrick jerked around. Leanna had sneaked up behind him again. How did the woman do that? She moved more silently than those ghosts she claimed to like.

She petted Diablo and stroked the white blaze down the bridge of his nose, easily dodging an attempted nip of the horse's teeth.

"I don't care," the boy argued. "He's big and I want a horse bigger than my sister's."

Ahhh, if there was one thing Patrick had more than his share of it was competitive spirit. He'd had a hard time getting his father's attention, but it hadn't kept him from trying. More often than not, his escapades had blown up in his face—which was why he was working so danged hard to prove his worth to his father now.

Leanna scratched behind Diablo's ears and stroked the Appaloosa's neck, earning herself a pal for life. "Then we'll have to ask Patrick if he has a bigger horse on the ranch that isn't so hard to handle."

Her enjoyment in stroking the animal sent his mind down the wrong path. Yanking it back, he rubbed his chin and tried to think about horses instead of soft hands and a tender touch or just how darn close he'd come to kissing her in his room this morning. That little sparring match had turned him on like nobody's business.

Nuts. Yeah, he was losing it.

"Tell you what, kiddo, if you think you can handle it, I'll put you on the biggest horse on the place."

Leanna's smile could've stopped a stampede, and the look in her eyes made him feel like a superhero.

Tim puffed his scrawny chest. "Sure I can."

"Well, come on. Goliath's so big he used to pull the dude ranch chuck wagon." He led the way to the pasture, opened the gate and whistled.

The twenty-year-old retired draft horse perked up his ears and jogged right up to them. Goliath was so tall Patrick could barely see over his withers, and Tim could almost walk under the horse's belly without bending over. Somebody sometime had trained him to saddle.

For about thirty seconds Tim looked doubtful, and then he whooped and hollered, waving his arms and kicking up dust. Most horses would've spooked, but Goliath just glanced at the kid and then returned to grazing. Despite his size, Goliath was, bar none, the gentlest horse on the spread.

Leanna's teeth dug into her plump bottom lip. The silent laughter glimmering in her eyes hit Patrick like a kick in the gut. How in the hell had he ever thought she was an uptight stick-in-the-mud?

The gentle nudge of Goliath's face against his back nearly knocked him off his feet. He regained his balance. Heat climbed his neck. He was too damned old to be sidetracked by a good set of lips. Even if he would be kissing them in four days. *Hell.*

He tried to adjust his jeans without being obvious, and cleared his throat. "How about sitting up on Goliath with Tim while I lead him around to the saddling rail?"

"Sure. Could you lead him closer to the fence so I can climb on?" She turned toward the rails.

He caught her hand and pulled her back, then dropped it when he realized what he'd done. The last thing he needed to do was feed his illogical fascination with her by touching her more than absolutely necessary. "I'll give you a leg up."

After hooking the lead line onto Goliath's halter, he bent and wrapped his hands around Leanna's calf and found it surprisingly muscular. He should have known her muscles were tight and well formed since he'd seen her naked....

Well, there was a detour his mind didn't need. With the sudden surge of testosterone in his blood he'd be lucky if he didn't toss her clear across the pasture. "Ready, set—"

Laying a hand on his shoulder, she protested, "Patrick, I'm too heavy."

"Go."

Up she went, settling in on Goliath's wide back like a pro. Patrick caught himself admiring the sleek line of her thighs and calves as she positioned herself. Leanna had the seat of an experienced rider. He'd always had a weakness for gals who knew what to do with a good piece of horseflesh, but he'd always avoided the ones who were good with kids like he would a rabid animal. Leanna had the markings of both.

She held out her arms for Tim, reminding him that he was supposed to be *working* instead of daydreaming. He forced his attention back to business. "Okay, Tim, you ride in front of Leanna until we get a saddle on this rogue."

He hefted the kid and gathered a handful of mane. "Latch on here. Until you have reins, this is your handle."

He led Goliath around the barn to the saddle rail where the other dudes had paired up with staff to receive instruction on the grooming and saddling of their mounts. Eyebrows lifted. They'd never used Goliath as a mount before, but it beat the heck out of letting the kid get hurt.

"Ease off, Tim." He held up his arms and the kid

vaulted off. No surprise there. The boy was a wiry little bundle of energy. Patrick caught him and set him on the ground. "Head on over to Toby and ask him to rustle up a saddle for Goliath."

The kid sprinted off and Patrick turned back to Leanna. She'd already swung her leg over to dismount. He moved forward to help her, but she moved faster than he anticipated. Instead of catching her waist and easing her down, his fingers brushed the sides of her breasts. She ended up pinned between him and the horse with her fanny snug in his crotch.

He yanked his hands away, cursed silently and stepped back. Usually he was a coordinated guy, but with Leanna he felt like a clumsy fool. "'Scuse me."

She spun around, tipping her head back to pin him with a wary gaze. The wariness slowly faded and awareness arched between them. He wished he could call it something else, but he was too experienced to misname the fireworks exploding in his bloodstream. And when she nibbled her lip like that…well, he wanted to do the same.

Never mind that Goliath's big body blocked them from the view of the others. He wasn't going to let himself be tempted into kissing her before Thursday even if one taste would probably cure his craving.

She wet her lips and he nearly groaned aloud. By the time he stepped around the saddle rail, his throat felt as tight as his jeans. "Thanks for helping. Tim's going to be a challenge."

She bent to brush the horse hair from the inner thighs of her jeans, and his palms tingled. "You're welcome. You're obviously well equipped to handle strong-willed boys."

He frowned. Was she insulting him? "How so?"

She shifted on her feet. "Your younger brothers."

"Right." She had him so danged worked up he'd forgotten he had younger brothers. Ridiculous. He was thirty-six years old and as randy as a teen.

"I should get back to work." She turned to leave, patting Goliath's rump as she passed. The woman obviously loved horses.

"Leanna, why don't you join us later for the evening trail ride?" He stifled a groan and wished the words back. For crying out loud, what was he thinking? He was hanging on by a thread here. The last thing he needed to do was add moonlight and a crackling fire into the mix.

Excitement sparkled in her eyes. "I really shouldn't. I have chores to do over at your place."

He had the perfect excuse to rescind the invitation, but he didn't, for some damned fool reason. "I'll drive you back after supper."

She wavered, but he could see by the way she looked over the horses that she wanted to go.

He'd feel like Scrooge if he backed out now. "Toby tells some killer ghost stories around the campfire."

She grinned and nodded. "Count me in."

And count him out of his mind, because his hammering heart meant he was looking forward to her company.

Five

Goose bumps danced across Leanna's skin.

Thunder rumbled in the distance, and the campfire crackled. Dark clouds obscured the moon, adding to the eerie ambiance. Toby, the trail boss, built to the climax of his ghost story and finished with a flourish.

A touch on her arm made her jump and squeal. She jerked around to find Patrick crouched beside her.

He frowned and tipped his head back to look at the sky. "Storm's supposed to keep to the east of us, but I'm beginning to have my doubts."

"How will you get everyone back if it rains?" A gust of wind blew a strand of her hair across his lips and when she reached to pull it back she brushed his skin. He needed a shave. His darkly bristled jaw grazed her fingertip and made her shiver.

Patrick sucked in a sharp breath and stood abruptly. Leanna straightened beside him. She curled her tingling fingers and shoved her hands into her pockets. He jerked his head, indicating they leave the campfire to talk. She followed him into the shadows beneath the trees.

"We don't. These folks paid to experience the cowboy life. The good and bad. A little rain won't hurt 'em. The tents are waterproof and on high ground. The horses are safe in the lean-to."

"What can I do to help you batten down the hatches, or whatever it is you do out here?"

"Gather anything that might blow away. Make sure bedrolls and anything that shouldn't get wet are inside a tent."

She saluted and clicked her heels. "You're the boss."

His dark eyes pinned her in place, giving no clue to his response to her sassy reply. "Don't forget it."

Another gust blew her hair into her eyes. He lifted his hand and tucked it behind her ear. Her heart pounded, and her skin tingled as if someone had poured fizzy peroxide over it. And then he clenched his fist, spun on his heel and walked away.

While Toby told another cowboy tale, Leanna scurried around tidying up. The strange feelings popping inside her like the popcorn in the metal popper the cook held over the fire were a sure sign that her attraction to Patrick was growing. Bad news.

As if someone had opened the floodgates on a dam, the rain poured. Dudes and staff raced to their shelters.

She hadn't planned on staying the night, and she didn't have a tent of her own. Who could she barge in on? For ten seconds she stood in the soaking rain and tried to remember which tent belonged to the female staff members while the rain glued her clothes to her skin.

"Come on." Patrick clamped a hand around her forearm and hustled her into a small one-man tent set on the edge of the campsite. She fell to her knees and crawled though the zippered opening. He crowded in behind her. Their arms and legs bumped and tangled in the darkness.

"Sit tight, I'll light the lantern." He said the words just inches from her ear, setting her insides aquiver.

Rain beat down on the canvas, muffling any sounds of his movement, but she could feel the bunch and shift of his muscles against hers. The wick flickered to life, casting a spooky, wavering light over the tent. The space seemed tiny and intimate with the two of them huddled inside.

She blotted the water from her face with an unsteady hand. She could handle this. Attraction only became a problem when acted upon. And she wouldn't let attraction to Patrick lead her into a relationship. She knew how those ended.

He tossed his hat into the corner. "Give it a few minutes. When the storm blows over I'll drive you back to the house."

They sat facing in opposite directions, cross-legged, side by side, his hip to her knee. His shoulder and thigh touched and warmed hers.

"Okay."

"Your teeth are chattering."

They chattered because she was cold and nervous. How many of her teenage fantasies had included young Patrick and his tent? Even though she'd long since outgrown those adolescent fantasies, she hadn't forgotten them. Her pulse accelerated.

In one of her letters, Carolyn had told Arch how Patrick and Jack had argued. Jack had laid down the law saying that Patrick would abide by his rules as long as he lived under the Lander roof and ate at the Lander table. For the remainder of the summer, fourteen-year-old Patrick had lived in a tent a half mile from home. He'd hunted for his food and lived off the land.

Leanna had envied Patrick the ability to get away and stand on his own two feet. His strength and bravery had given her the courage to run away when her mother's lover had attacked her. As far as she knew, her mother hadn't looked for her. Tonya certainly hadn't protested when Arch had asked her to sign over guardianship a year later. Of course, once millionaire Arch had taken Leanna under his wing, her mother had become very friendly.

"You weren't kidding when you said you liked ghost stories. You hung on Toby's words." She could barely hear Patrick's quiet voice over the pounding rain and distant thunder.

"Arch used to tell me bedtime stories."

Patrick stiffened. The lines in his face deepened in revulsion.

"Get your mind out of the gutter. It's not what you think. My mother liked to party. She'd stay out all hours of the night and sometimes she didn't come home for days. Arch saw how I worried and tried to distract me. At first he just bought me books. When he realized I wasn't a good reader, he read to me. The scary stories were our favorites."

Her eyes burned, and she wanted to cry. She'd had so little time to mourn Arch and even less time to come to terms with the upheaval of her own life before the executrix duties had begun.

When this job ended she didn't know where she'd go or what she'd do. If her mother stayed sober, then maybe she'd be able to find an apartment for the two of them and finish college.

Her throat tightened. "Arch could do the character's voices like you wouldn't believe."

Patrick's face remained tense. "My mother used to tell me ghost stories, too. She'd put me in the car and drive to the Pink Palace, which had been made into a B and B. The legend is that the madam became a madam because she couldn't have children. I always thought Mom wanted to give me to the madam's ghost. God knows, I was a handful."

Leanna opened her mouth to tell him his mother had been looking for Arch and then closed it. This wasn't the time or place to tell him that Arch had promised to come back for them when he could afford to support them. Patrick deserved privacy—not a camp full of dudes—when she told him the truth.

But she understood how a parent's actions could make a child feel unwanted. *Unloved.* Leanna laid a hand on his arm and caught his gaze in the flickering light. "I'm sorry."

His big hand covered hers and quicker than a flash of lightning the atmosphere inside the tent changed. She'd never been sexually attracted to anyone before, but she'd be a fool to misname the tension coiling low in her abdomen and making it difficult to catch her breath.

Patrick's pupils dilated and his lips parted. His gaze dropped to her mouth and his fingers tightened over hers.

"Patrick—" She couldn't manage more than a whisper.

"Hell, let's get it over with. I'm tired of thinking about it."

A shiver raced over her skin. It wasn't caused by her wet clothes or the wind rattling the tent. "You've been thinking about—" she swallowed hard and wet her lips "—kissing me?"

He scrubbed a hand over his face and admitted with obvious reluctance, "Yeah."

He smoothed his fingers over her damp hair, making her want to close her eyes and purr. She'd been over her crush on him for years. How dangerous could one kiss be? She was afraid to find out. Curling her fingers around his biceps, she tried to find the words to explain why this wasn't a good idea, but his lips sealed hers before she could voice her objections.

His gentleness surprised the protest right out of her. From the fire in his eyes she'd expected to be consumed in one big gulp, but he sipped from her lips, nuzzling and teasing, touching and withdrawing, until she tightened her grip and leaned closer.

His fingers tangled in her hair and he angled his head to deepen the kiss. She tasted a hint of after-dinner coffee when his tongue touched hers. The slight prickle of his evening beard teased her cheek and his heart pounded beneath her palm. Her own pulse sprinted to catch up.

Kissing Patrick felt so good. Could it possibly be wrong? Could he be the kind of man she'd dreamed of meeting? Tentatively she kissed him back.

He rewarded her with a deep groan and pulled her closer. Her breast pressed against his chest. His warmth permeated her damp shirt and licked through her like wildfire. Desire kindled inside her and her control slipped. When his slick tongue twined with hers and his free hand stroked down her spine to curve over her bottom, she lost all sense of time and place.

She savored his taste, his texture, his heat. He shifted his hands to her waist and lifted her into his lap. She gasped in surprise, but didn't protest when his arms banded around her.

Everything spun, swirled and drifted around her while she stayed firmly seated in a cradle of his tense thigh muscles like a character trapped in a snow globe. Overwhelmed by the sensation, she would have pulled away, but his hand skated from her waist to her breast. He cupped her with a hot palm, and her objections scattered. The scrape of his thumbnail across her tight nipple sent a ripple of pleasure through her like nothing she'd ever experienced.

She'd shared kisses before, but the men in her past had been takers and easy to resist. Patrick seemed determined to give as much pleasure as he received. He seduced her with his touch, his gentleness, his hunger.

The storm inside raged fiercer than the one pounding on the tent. She grew greedy for more. Lifting her arms, she twined her arms around his neck and threaded her fingers through the springy strands at his nape.

His shoulders stiffened, and he lifted his head a fraction of an inch. His panting breaths mingled with hers and his burning gaze inflamed her. "Leanna, we're crossing deep waters here. I have a feeling you're in over your head."

Reality slapped her sober. She didn't want to make the same mistake her mother often did of confusing a man's lust with love. Struggling to get out of Patrick's arms, her elbow caught him in the belly. He oofed out a grunt and tightened his arms, molding her tight against the hot steel of his chest. A burst of panic shot through her veins and she struggled harder.

"Whoa. Easy, now. No need to maim me. I'll turn you loose, but I'd like to keep my ribs intact." He lifted her from his lap and sat her back on the bedroll.

Shudders racked her, but it wasn't because she was cold. It was fear interwoven with the cooling remnants of need. For a split second when Patrick had held her tight, she'd had a flashback to the shower scene seven years ago, but that had quickly passed. The need hadn't. It lingered in her system, like a ravenous hunger gnawing her insides, making her long to throw caution to the winds. That scared her. She knew where that road led. It wasn't a trip she wanted to take. She'd always promised herself that she'd never settle for less than an honorable man even if that meant she'd never have a family of her own—the one thing she wanted more than anything.

Patrick swore, dug around in his bag and pulled out a dry T-shirt. "Put this on before you catch a chill."

He glanced at the luminescent face of his watch and turned off the lantern. She could feel his movements, but in the darkness she couldn't see him.

"We can't drive until the rain lets up. The path will be a muddy mess. I'm going to catch some sleep. I suggest you do the same."

Leanna hugged the T-shirt to her chest and wondered what she'd do now that she knew her crush on Patrick had never died. Falling for him would only end in heartache, and if she followed her mother's pattern, only alcohol or drugs would dull the pain.

"Put on the dry shirt or I'll put it on you myself."

She didn't dare risk his touch again with her body still clamoring for more and her mental health at stake.

In the inky darkness she couldn't tell the back of the shirt from the front without feeling for the tag. Patrick wouldn't be able to see any better. She quickly unbuttoned the wet dude ranch uniform shirt and peeled it off. She pulled the T-shirt over her chilled flesh, and warmth seeped through her.

"Stretch out and get some sleep." The tension in his voice was unmistakable.

Reluctantly she did as he ordered, turning her back on him. Her bottom nudged his. The seams of their back pockets snagged against each other. He jerked away, muttering under his breath.

Moving to the very edge of the bedroll, she closed her eyes and said a prayer of thanks for Arch's firm beliefs in natural medicine. She ran through her entire repertoire of calming biofeedback methods before her tense muscles began to unwind.

When she was on the verge of sleep, a thought crept into her mind. If Patrick was really the womanizer he and the crew claimed, she'd be naked and flat on her back by now. Instead, he'd gallantly denied his own pleasure and offered her the opportunity to change her mind.

Patrick Lander was definitely living up to his mother's expectations. Arch would be proud.

And she was in trouble, because it looked like Patrick Lander might be the kind of man she'd always wanted.

Patrick mentally beat himself black and blue until the storm broke shortly after midnight.

Stupid. Yep. What kind of fool played with gasoline and a lit match? Him, obviously. He knew he was attracted to Leanna and that she was off-limits. And what did he do? Drag her into his tent. Stupid. But she'd looked like a drowned kitten out there in the rain.

Inexperienced. Yep. He could taste it in her kiss. Feel it in her tentative touch.

Willing. Oh, yeah. If his conscience had let him, he'd have invaded more than Leanna's sweet mouth tonight, and his aching and throbbing body knew it.

Lecher. Yep. He was a jackass to even consider taking what Leanna offered. Her life had been rough enough without a greedy bastard like him taking advantage.

Spooked. Something about the kiss had spooked her. Not during the kiss, but after. He was used to making women tremble with desire, but need hadn't made Leanna shake. Her fear had been palpable in the muggy tent. He'd bet a month's salary that it hadn't been fear of him. So what was it?

He eased over to face her but couldn't see her in the inky darkness. Didn't need to. He could hear her even breathing. She slept just inches away.

Smell her. Oh, yeah. He inhaled deeply. Her soap, sunshine and vanilla scent was headier than any perfume he'd ever come across.

Touch her. He didn't dare, but he didn't have any problem recalling the silkiness of her hair, the softness of her skin, the weight of her breast in his palm, or the sweet pressure of her hip against his groin.

Taste her. He licked his dry lips, and her flavor lingered. Worse, he hungered for more.

Aw, hell, he was the one in over his head, swept away with lust for a gal years too young for him. One who wasn't being straight with him. His mother had kept too many secrets, told too many lies for him to want to tangle with dishonesty again.

And then of course there was Amanda, his one venture into the insanity of love. He'd been a blind fool. Amanda had strung him along, letting him believe they needed to keep their love a secret until he'd earned her father's respect. He'd bent over backward trying to do just that. All the while she'd been two-timing him with his older brother.

Once she'd trapped Caleb into marriage with a false pregnancy, she'd dumped Patrick like a load of manure. When he'd confronted her she'd said Caleb had better prospects. He, on the other hand, was nothing more than a good time and a good lay. She'd promised her marriage wouldn't change that part of their relationship, but he drew the line at sleeping with another man's wife—especially his brother's.

Dishonest women. He'd learned the hard way to steer clear of 'em. Until he figured out the real reason Leanna had packed all her belongings and come to Texas, he'd have to find a way to keep his mind *and his hands* off her.

Easier said than done.

Leanna waved goodbye to Toby and let herself into the Lander house. She'd awoken this morning to a muggy and empty tent. As soon as she'd stepped outside Toby had told her he had orders to deliver her to Crooked Creek.

Patrick was nowhere to be found and that suited her just fine. She had an hour to shower, change and get back to the Double C, and she needed every second of that time to regroup. She wanted Patrick's friendship and his trust, but how could she gain those without risking a repeat of last night?

"Got rained on, did ya?" Jack Lander called from

the kitchen table. His sharp gaze skimmed over Patrick's shirt—the one on her back...and hers...in her hand.

"Yes."

"We needed it." He stood slowly, stiffly, and carried his plate to the sink. "Came down too fast, and most of it ran off, but it's a start."

Too fast... Yes, things had definitely moved too fast last night. "If you'll excuse me, I...need to get ready for work."

He waved her on, and Leanna jogged up the stairs. After a quick shower she combed her hair and pulled it back into a no-nonsense clip. She hoped her baggy jeans and shirt would make it clear that she was not interested in luring Patrick.

She gathered her dirty clothes and Patrick's clothes from the bathroom hamper and then collected Jack's from his room. She turned to go, but a photo on the bedside table stopped her. The dark-haired, dark-eyed beauty had to be Carolyn. She moved closer and picked up the frame. Arch hadn't had any photos, but he'd talked about her often, leading Leanna to wonder about the woman who'd captured and held Arch's heart for a lifetime.

Patrick had obviously inherited his coloring from his mother. He had the same glossy hair and the same rich-brown eyes with a let's-play glint.

"Pretty, ain't she?" Jack said from the door. He sounded a little winded from climbing the stairs.

Leanna quickly set the picture back on his night table. "Yes, she is. Patrick's mother?"

He moved slowly into the room and lowered himself into the upholstered chair in the corner. "Yep. Carolyn was like a wild mustang, beautiful and strong-willed, and every man who met her wanted to own her. I made the mistake of trying to corral her and succeeded...for a while. But you can't keep the wild ones penned. In the end, she busted the fence and ran off.''

He looked Leanna over and added, ''Patrick takes after her.''

It was a warning, plain and simple, but an unnecessary one. She wasn't here to *corral* Patrick. If anything, his inheritance from Arch would free him to pursue whatever he wanted in life.

''You must have loved her very much.''

''Love don't die just because one of you's gone.''

He still loved Carolyn. Her heart sank. Would the news that she'd been unfaithful hurt him? Her conscience taunted her. The man had already lost his wife. Could she destroy the memories he had of her? How could she not? The best she could do was break it to him and Patrick gently before the will was filed and the press vultures caught the scent of Arch Golden's biggest secret.

''What kind of job did you have out in California that led you to a dude ranch in Texas?''

Her heart stuttered. ''I was a hostess and a social secretary for an actor.''

''Anybody I've heard of?''

She wouldn't lie. ''Arch Golden.''

If he knew about Arch and Carolyn he didn't let on. ''Must be a world of difference between here and there.''

''Yes, but I like it here very much. I'd better get the laundry started and get over to the Double C.''

''When you're ready, I'll give you a ride.''

''Thanks.'' She carried the clothes downstairs and mechanically filled the washing machine.

What quality made Carolyn Lander the kind of woman two men had loved for a lifetime while her own mother had been the type men quickly tired of?

Which type was she? With a sinking feeling in the pit of her stomach, Leanna feared she was her mother's daughter and completely forgettable and unlovable.

What kind of man was Patrick? With two fathers who'd loved for a lifetime and an unforgettable mother, she bet he was the forever kind of man beneath his charming exterior—the kind of man she'd once dreamed of marrying back in her adolescence. Back then she'd wanted more than anything to belong somewhere and to someone. But now, knowing her mother's weakness, she was afraid to risk it.

The cow got by him, and his horse nearly dumped him in the process. Patrick fought for balance.

Dammit. He had to get his head back in the game. He was supposed to be teaching the greenhorns how to cut cattle out of the herd, not how to land face first in the corral. Instead, he was reliving a kiss that shouldn't have happened.

Toby rode up beside him. "You okay?"

"Yeah. Sun got in my eyes."

Toby wasn't stupid. He smirked. "Uh-huh."

Patrick motioned to the teenage girl waiting her turn. She moved into the herd and singled out her selection. He watched the kid fight the horse and called out, "Sit back and let the horse do the work. Learn the way he moves and move with him. That's it."

"She's cute," Toby said.

He pretended ignorance. "Who?"

Toby gave him a you're-dumber-than-a-rock stare. "Leanna."

"I guess." He could still taste her, even though he'd brushed his teeth twice this morning. He'd waited until he was sure she'd left the house before returning home to shower, but her scent had lingered in the bathroom they shared.

His shower had been a cold one—just what he needed after a long night of tossing and turning on the hard ground. His muscles were achy and sluggish.

It was stupid—*danged* stupid—to get hung up on her when absolutely nothing was going to happen between them. That kiss last night had surprised him—more because he'd stopped than because of the rockets she'd set off in his bloodstream.

Out of the corner of his eye he saw her leave one cabin and enter the next, and just like that he recalled the sweet way she'd kissed him back, the way her fingers had tangled in his hair, the way she'd whimpered into his mouth when he caressed her breast. His blood headed south.

One of the guests, a single guy named Gabe, broke away from the group and followed Leanna inside the cabin. Patrick waited for her to come out. Minutes passed and still no sign of Leanna. His horse shifted nervously beneath him, and Patrick realized his tensed muscles were confusing the animal.

"I'll be back." He signaled one of the other crew members to take over, rode out of the corral and right up to the cabin door. Dismounting, he strode inside.

Leanna and Gabe stood on opposite sides of the bed, a corner of the sheet in each of their hands, laughing. Patrick's temper soared. She'd broken a rule and exposed herself to a potentially dangerous situation.

"Leanna, outside. Now." He could barely choke the words out through the emotion clogging his throat.

Gabe looked anxious. "Hey, man, we're just talking about California. I did my undergrad studies at UCLA."

Patrick held the cabin door opened and waited. His muscles knotted with tension. Leanna walked toward him but called to Gabe, "We can talk during dinner."

The hell they would. "In the office."

He ate up the distance to the main house in long strides while he struggled with his temper. What was his problem? He was the easy-going type. He never lost his cool. So how could he explain the fury and the fear in his blood? He stomped into the house, down the hall, past the painters and into the office. As soon as Leanna crossed the threshold, he slammed the door so hard he'd probably have to replace the hinges.

Leanna eyed him warily. "Patrick, we were only talking."

"You broke the rules." He ground out the words through his clenched jaw.

"I was perfectly safe. Half the staff is within shouting distance."

She just didn't get it. He yanked her into his arms and ground his mouth over hers. For all of ten seconds surprise stiffened her spine, and then she opened her mouth beneath his and curved her body against him.

His anger evaporated like water in a hot skillet when her lips parted and her silky tongue tentatively touched his. Desire sizzled though his veins with an intensity that set him back on his heels. He jerked away even though the temptation to surrender to the need tying his gut in knots pulled at him.

Pacing to the window, he watched the goings-on outside without interest. "I didn't hear you screaming."

"Was I supposed to?"

He turned to glare at her. She lowered the fingers covering her mouth, and guilt kicked him in the teeth. Her lips were already swelling. He'd been too rough.

Hell, he shouldn't have kissed her at all.

"You weren't screaming because you couldn't, even if you'd wanted to. I had your hands trapped and your mouth covered. If I'd wanted to take you right there on that desk you wouldn't have been able to stop me."

She snatched a quick breath. The color in her cheeks fluctuated between pale and pink as her gaze darted to the desk and back to him. But the frown between her brows told him she still didn't get it.

"Six years ago a woman was raped in one of the cabins—with half the crew in hearing range. Fifty feet away and we missed the whole thing. We didn't see the dude follow her into the cabin, and we never heard her scream. Because she couldn't. He bound her mouth with his bandanna and raped her. On my watch."

Guilt burned him like acid. He'd let the woman down by failing to protect her, and he'd let down Charlie, the dude ranch owner at the time, by failing in his duties.

Compassion and understanding softened Leanna's expression. He closed his eyes against it only to open them again when her hand settled on his forearm. "You're not a superhero, Patrick. You can't see through walls, and unless you're psychic you can't read thoughts or predict the future."

"A woman's life changed forever that day, and it was my fault. I won't let it happen again."

Her fingers tightened. His mind shifted away from the fierce protectiveness he'd felt for her today to the way she'd melted against him and the hunger that incinerated him without warning. His throat and jeans tightened. He shook his head, trying to clear it.

"When a guy like me looks at you and starts having the thoughts I'm having, you're supposed to slap him."

Confusion darkened her eyes. "What do you mean by a guy like you?"

He might as well lay it on the line. He wanted her, but he wasn't in for the long haul. "I don't have a faithful bone in my body."

"You're loyal to the ones you care about."

Was she serious? He barked out a harsh laugh. "Don't fool yourself."

"Aren't you working overtime to take care of Brooke and Caleb's place?"

He frowned. "That's different. I like the dude ranch."

"You don't worry about Jack?"

"He's my father, dammit." Patrick put the width of the desk between them. Why was she trying to paint him as some kind of hero?

"You've had ample opportunity to take advantage of me, Patrick, and you haven't. I can't say the same for some of the men my mother used to bring around."

The protective burn rekindled in his gut. He wanted to pound anyone who'd hurt her. "I'm not some damned saint."

"No one expects you to be, and just for the record, if I'd wanted to stop you I would have kneed your groin, stomped your instep, and jabbed my fingers in your eyes. If that hadn't worked I'd have shoved your nose into your brain."

She voiced the words in a normal tone, but the fortitude in her eyes and in her jaw were pure steel.

A vision of her naked in the wash stall flashed in

his mind. He'd assumed her well-defined muscles were those of an athlete. It had never entered his mind that she might stay in shape for self-defense. "Why do you know how to do that?"

"My mother brought home some real losers. I took free self-defense classes at the Y."

What kind of life had she lived? He rubbed a hand over his face. "None of this was in your file."

She rolled her eyes. "I looked at that file, and it only goes back to the second time I moved in with Arch. It doesn't mention the eleven different men my mother lived with before I turned fifteen. It doesn't mention the eight months I lived on the streets after I ran away."

His chest hurt. "Why'd you run?"

"Because the streets were safer."

His home had always been a haven. No matter how badly he'd screwed up or how hard his father had come down on him, he'd never feared for his safety. He'd taken that for granted. Never again. "Leanna—"

She held up a hand, moved to the door and yanked it open. "One of the maids is out sick today, and I'm way behind schedule. If I want a lunch break I need to get back to work. Are we through here?"

She didn't wait for his answer, and it was just as well. He didn't have one. He liked women. Hell, he loved women. But he'd never had one confuse him the way Leanna did. She was soft and innocent one minute and a streetwise fighter the next. Darned if he didn't like contradiction.

He wanted to take care of her, and he'd never felt that way about anyone other than family.

It scared the hell out of him.

Six

She was her mother's daughter.

Leanna looked in the bathroom mirror and touched her lips. She could remember the taste and texture of Patrick's kiss even though hours had passed. The lingering ache in her abdomen alarmed her.

She wanted Patrick. The sexual chemistry between them was undeniable, but his protectiveness was the clincher. Patrick Lander was an honorable man.

Turning on the bathroom faucet, she splashed cold water on her face. It would serve no purpose to resurrect her crush or to fall in love with him. She needed to stop these strange feelings from going any further. She'd do the job she came to do and go back to her mother, her obligations and her education.

Tonight she'd tell Patrick about Arch. If he hated her for shattering his world, then he wouldn't keep tempting her to break her own heart and risk her sanity by falling for him.

Footsteps ascended the stairs. She knew it wasn't Jack because Jack had gone out, giving her the perfect opportunity to talk to Patrick. She met him at the top of the stairs.

He stopped. "I'm sorry for jumping all over you today."

Taken aback by the apology, she blinked at him. "No apology needed. Can we, um, talk for a few minutes?"

He hesitated. "What is it, kid?"

"Would you stop with the kid thing already? I've figured out that you use it every time you're trying to put up a wall between us, but it's not going to work. I have something I need to show you in my room."

She returned to her room. A few heartbeats later she heard his footsteps following her. The fresh outdoor scent of him filled her senses, and she struggled to keep her mind on business.

He looked back down the hall. "Have you seen Dad?"

"He's spending the night with his granddaughters. He said to tell you he'd be home by lunchtime tomorrow."

He didn't look pleased. "Brand and Toni's twins. Just a few months old. I'm their godfather."

Yet another sign that he'd lived up to his mother's expectations. "I'm sure you're a great one."

"Don't put your faith in the wrong man."

"I don't think I am. You talk the talk of a charmer, Patrick, but you don't walk the walk. You care too much about your family to be a selfish person."

A dull flush rose on his cheeks. "I'm no Prince Charming."

"Of course not. The prince was a fictional character."

He shifted from one boot to the other. "Are you trying to get me into the sack, angel? Because if you are, I'll remind you that I'm not somebody you can rely on for the long haul."

His bluntness erased the practiced speech from her mind. Tension spiraled through her at the thought of making love with him, which was exactly why she needed to hurry up and tell him about his father—his *real* father. If only she could remember what she'd planned to say....

"Obviously, your brother believes differently or he wouldn't have entrusted you with his daughters."

"Leanna—"

She held up a hand. "That's not what I needed to talk to you about. I have something to show you."

His brows rose and his lips twisted in a naughty grin.

"I don't mean skin," she said quickly.

Her heart pounding, Leanna crossed to the closet, opened the door and reached for the box she'd hidden inside. She set it on the mattress in front of him and sat back down.

She took a deep breath and traced the carved initials on the lid. Her next words would change Patrick's world forever, but she'd promised Arch and *she* never broke promises.

"Patrick, I feel like I've known you forever."

Patrick studied the carved wooden box and wondered if Leanna had stolen it from Golden's house. It looked expensive. "That's flattering, but you've only known me five days."

If offer card is missing write to: Silhouette Reader Service, 3010 Walden Ave., P.O. Box 1867, Buffalo NY 14240-1867

NO POSTAGE
NECESSARY
IF MAILED
IN THE
UNITED STATES

BUSINESS REPLY MAIL

FIRST-CLASS MAIL   PERMIT NO. 717-003   BUFFALO, NY

POSTAGE WILL BE PAID BY ADDRESSEE

SILHOUETTE READER SERVICE
3010 WALDEN AVE
PO BOX 1867
BUFFALO NY 14240-9952

Do You Have the LUCKY KEY?

Scratch the gold areas with a coin. Then check below to see the books and gift you can get!

PLAY THE Lucky Key Game

and you can get

FREE BOOKS and a FREE GIFT!

326 SDL DVAE   225 SDL DVAU

FIRST NAME	LAST NAME

ADDRESS

APT.#   CITY

STATE / PROV.   ZIP/POSTAL CODE

2 free books plus a free gift   1 free book

2 free books   Try Again!

Visit us online at www.eHarlequin.com

DETACH AND MAIL CARD TODAY!

(S-D-10/03)

"No, we met five days ago, but I've known you—
known about you—since I was twelve."

That sounded a little creepy. He didn't know why
she'd invited him into her room, but he sure as hell
knew he should get up and leave. Now. He stood.

"This humidor contains letters from your mother."

His muscles froze. "My mother's dead."

"I know, but before she died, she wrote seventeen
letters to Arch Golden."

His mother had been a big Golden fan. Her claim to
fame was that she'd worked with the actor at the local
theater. She'd made Patrick sit through every two-bit
film Golden had played in, and she'd often read to him
from her collection of magazine and newspaper articles
mentioning Golden.

"Why would she write letters to a movie star?"

"To tell him about the son they shared."

The hair on the back of his neck stood up. He backed
toward the door. "It's late. We—"

"You're that son, Patrick."

Patrick's knees locked. Was this a sick joke? He
looked over his shoulder to see if his brothers or his
buddies were lurking in the hall, waiting to laugh at
him. They weren't.

Leanna opened the box, and he recognized his
mother's distinctive loopy handwriting on the flowery
stationery she'd favored. His gut clenched, and his
heart beat like a jackhammer. "I don't know what that
crazy man told you, but—"

"Arch didn't tell me. Your mother's letters did. She
wrote one when she found out she was pregnant with
you and one each year on your birthday. And she sent
pictures."

She nudged the box toward him, and Patrick backed away like it was a coiled rattler.

"I didn't find the courage to ask Arch about his love child until I moved back in with him six years ago, and then he told me about you and how much he missed being a part of your life."

Love child? Him? No way.

Memories flashed through his mind of his mother whining because she didn't think his father paid her enough attention, or conversely, that he smothered her by never letting her leave the ranch alone. He remembered the arguments when she'd suggested taking a part-time job because money was tight, and his father's reply, "Remember what happened last time." She'd promised it wouldn't happen again. Eventually she'd talked her way into another part-time job, because she'd always been able to talk his father into anything.

But his memories meant nothing. They sure as hell didn't lend credence to Leanna's ridiculous story.

Jack Lander was his father.

Patrick Lander was the second of four sons born to the not-so-happy couple. *Wasn't he?*

Nausea curdled in his stomach.

Leanna lifted the first letter in the stack and read, "My dearest Arch, I miss you unbearably, but today I discovered a balm for my misery. Our meetings at Swain's resulted in a wondrous gift. I'm carrying your child."

No! Shoving a hand into his hair, Patrick massaged the ache building behind his temple. "Swain's?"

"Yes, evidently, your mother met Arch at a friend's."

His thoughts scrambled. "Swain's Pink Palace."

Her brows rose. "The haunted rooming house?"

"Penny Swain still owns the place. She changed the name when she put up a new sign a while back. Fewer words cost less money." He backed toward the door. "This is nuts. I don't know where you got this cockamamie story, but I'm not—"

"You are, Patrick. You're Arch Golden's son. And you're his heir."

He staggered to the dresser and leaned against it. "You're wrong."

"A simple DNA test will prove it—if you don't believe your own mother." She nudged the box a few inches closer.

A cold sweat beaded his forehead and upper lip. His hands felt clammy and his head spun. *Crazy.*

Jack Lander was his father.

What if he wasn't? What if this insane tale wasn't Hollywood hype?

"Patrick?" Leanna's soft voice and her gentle hand on his arm brought him back. He studied her direct gaze, looking for a sign that she was lying or just yanking his chain. Nobody loved a practical joke better than he did. But this one was pretty damned sick.

Her hazel eyes were sincere. "I think you should read your mother's letters and prepare your family before the paparazzi gets wind of the news. I'm the executrix of Arch's estate, and I can tell you it's only a matter of time before the will becomes public record."

She wasn't kidding. She was wrong, but Leanna obviously believed this insane soap opera story.

"I know that kiss was good, kid, but I didn't expect it to make you delirious."

She winced at his sarcasm and her cheeks flushed. "Patrick—"

"I'll see you in the morning. Tomorrow's lessons are castrating and branding. Dress to get dirty."

Before she could say another word, he stepped out of the room and pulled the door closed behind him. With his head reeling, he staggered to his room and shut and locked his door.

There was no doubt that his mother had been a cheater. As a kid he'd heard the rumors. They'd been confirmed when she'd gone off to Mexico with a man and been killed there in a car crash. He wouldn't be surprised to learn that she'd had an affair with the actor, too.

But to pass off one man's kid as another's? His mother wouldn't stoop so low. His father wouldn't have tolerated it.

Would he?

Pacing to the window, Patrick stared out into the darkness. He'd always thought his father had been tougher on him than on his brothers. Was it because he resented raising another man's bastard?

Nah. Leanna was wrong.

She had to be. Or else his entire life had been a lie.

Patrick took one look at her outfit and frowned. "I thought I told you to dress to get dirty."

Leanna glanced down at her embroidered white peasant top and matching drawstring pants. "You did, but Brooke never helped with the castrating or branding."

Patrick closed the truck's door and fastened his seatbelt. "Nope. Some women don't have the stomach for it."

Leanna ignored his challenge—for now. Next week, she'd prove she was woman enough for the job. "I'm taking the Jeep ride with the guests who want to take nature pictures.''

''Borrow one of Brooke's hats and wear sunscreen.''

Leanna was determined to confront him about the issue he'd avoided throughout breakfast. ''You left the letters in my room last night.''

He only paused a second before shoving the truck into gear and pulling onto the dirt road leading to the dude ranch. ''I'm not interested in fan mail my mother might have written.''

''They're more than fan mail, Patrick. They're love letters and…well, diaries, almost.''

He slammed on the brakes and jerked around to face her. ''Keep your crazy story to yourself.''

She knew the news of his paternity had to be hard for him to take. ''Patrick, the facts won't change if you ignore them. We don't have much time. The paparazzi will be on your doorstep as soon as they catch wind of this.''

He faced forward and put the truck into motion. His jaw and shoulders became rigid.

''You need to tell your family. Jack shouldn't be blindsided by the media. What if he doesn't know Carolyn was unfaithful?''

He kept his eyes on the road, but his knuckles turned white on the steering wheel, and a deep groove appeared beside his mouth. ''He knew.''

And Jack still loved her. Leanna laid a hand over her heart. What would it be like to be loved no matter how big your mistakes?

''What if he doesn't know you're not his biological son?''

''I am, dammit. Look at me. Look at him.''

''I have. You have your mother's coloring. I know

Jack is a brunet as well, but it's a different shade. And your bone structure is pure Arch.'' She pulled a photo from her pocket.

He swung forward as if she'd slapped him. ''Put that away. I don't want to see the pervert.''

''Arch wasn't a pervert. He was kind and generous and the closest thing to a father that I had.''

He glared at her. ''If he was so damned perfect then why did you freak out in the wash stall and when Warren flirted with you?''

Exhaling slowly, she closed her eyes and wet her lips. Fearing others would also believe she'd been a tease, she'd told no one but Arch. ''When I was fifteen my mother's lover snuck up on me when I was in the shower. He tried to rape me and would have succeeded if Mom hadn't forgotten her cigarettes and returned to the house.''

Patrick swore and the truck swerved on the dirt path when he swung around to look at her. ''Did they lock the bastard up?''

''No. He convinced my mother that I'd led him on. She chose to believe him rather than acknowledge that the scumbag would cheat on her. That's when I ran away.''

His language should have blistered the paint from the truck. It touched her that he not only believed her, he cared enough to be angry for her.

She reached out and laid a hand on his shoulder. The muscles bunched beneath her fingertips. ''Arch was a wonderful man. I wish you could have known him.''

His Adam's apple bobbed as he swallowed. ''Why are you doing this?''

''Because Arch asked me to find you and explain

why he never contacted you after your mother died. It
wasn't that he didn't love you—''

"He didn't even know me.''

She winced at the bitterness in his voice. "He knew
more about you than you think. I have a letter for you
from Arch.''

"Burn it.''

"You're his only living relative and his heir. You
can't ignore that. The press won't let you. You need
to decide what you're going to do with his estate.''

"I don't want it.''

"Arch's holdings are valued in the millions. You're
a millionaire, Patrick.''

"No, I'm not. I'm a dirt-poor rancher. Do whatever
you want with that bastard's estate. Keep it for yourself. Give it away. Hell, I don't care. He's not my father. It's not mine.''

"Arch wanted you to have—''

He braked hard and the truck skidded to a halt beside
the barn. He twisted in his seat. "Don't you get it? *If*
what you say is true, Golden didn't want anything to
do with me when he was alive. Now it's too late. So,
if unloading that estate is the only reason you took this
job then you might as well quit right now.''

She'd wanted to see if the only man worthy of her
trust and her respect had died or if Carolyn Lander had
raised her son to share his father's integrity. "It's not
the only reason.''

"Fine. Today's the dudes' last day. We want to
leave 'em beggin' to come back.'' He climbed out of
the truck and slammed the door. After snatching his
leather chaps from the bed of the truck, he strode toward the main house.

Leanna hustled after him, jogging to catch up. She

grabbed his arm. "Whether you want your inheritance or not, you have to tell your family. *Soon*, Patrick."

He parked his fists on his hips. "Tell me something. If he was like a father to you, then why didn't he leave his estate to *you*?"

Because even though Arch had loved her in his own way, she'd never been his flesh and blood. "I'm taken care of."

"He left you a chunk?"

"I'm being paid for acting as executrix of the estate."

"Millions?"

"No."

"Is that why you're here? You want more money? Maybe you want to be a millionaire's wife."

"*No!*"

"If a wedding ring is what you're looking for, kid, you won't get one from me. I don't do commitment."

She took a deep breath. Patrick was hurting and lashing out. He didn't know her well enough to know that money had never been an issue for her. Arch had known. "You need to consider Jack. He's ill. He works too hard. Just going up and down the stairs tires him."

His dark gaze bored into hers. "What in the hell do you think I am doing? My mother might have been a tramp, but he loved her. If I tell him your story—and I'm not saying I believe it—then every time he looks at me he'll be reminded that she didn't love him back."

"But she did."

"Cheating on him is a fine way to show it." He wiped a hand across his jaw. "Dad already thinks I'm the biggest screw-up in Texas and I can't blame him since I stayed in trouble most of my life, but do you want him to hate the sight of me, too?"

The hurt in his eyes made her own eyes sting. Her chest and throat ached. "He won't hate you, Patrick."

"And where will I live? If I'm not a Lander then I don't belong on Crooked Creek. But I sure as hell don't belong in *California*." He looked and sounded lost.

"You could buy your own place."

"I want to live here. With my family."

"They've loved you for thirty-six years. That won't change."

"Wrong. If what you say is true, then they don't even know who I am. Get the papers, Leanna. I'll sign everything over to you. You'll have your millions." He pivoted on his boot heel and left her.

She ran after him and stepped in his path. A few yards away dudes and staff gathered around the breakfast tables set up on the back porch of the main house. She whispered, "You can't just give away fifteen million dollars."

His eyes widened and then he scowled. "Watch me."

He tried to step around her, but she moved to block his way. "You have cars and homes and investments and employees to deal with."

"You're the executrix. You handle it."

"Okay. I'll make a deal with you. If you still want to give your inheritance away *after* you've read your mother's letters, I'll help you choose the charitable organizations. But first, you have to give me the chance to do what Arch asked me to do and that's to tell you about him and your mother."

"Forget it." His lips flattened in rejection.

Leanna knew she'd have to fight dirty. Her promise to Arch hinged on winning this fight. "Why? Are you afraid you might like the man who ignored you your entire life or, heaven forbid, understand his reasons?''

His jaw muscles knotted. "Don't play games with me, kid."

"I've already challenged and beaten you twice, cowboy. I think you're chicken. But face facts, Patrick, once the will is filed I'll have to call a press conference if you haven't already."

She turned and hurried up onto the back porch before he could reply. Unless she'd misjudged him, Patrick would read the letters before bedtime. Just to be sure, she'd leave the humidor in his room.

If she'd had doubts before, she now knew for certain that Patrick was the kind of man she'd once dreamed of meeting, of making a life with. He valued family above anything...

Even fifteen million dollars.

Too bad she couldn't have him.

The black hole in Patrick's chest threatened to consume him. He tossed the last letter back into the box.

He'd read each of his mother's letters; the first announcing her pregnancy, and sixteen more sent on each of his birthdays before she died. And then he'd read them a second time to make sure he hadn't misunderstood—*he hadn't*—or that his mother hadn't miscalculated her dates. She hadn't.

His gaze shifted from the photos of his childhood piled on his bed to those tucked around his mirror.

He wasn't Jack Lander's son. He swallowed hard.

He was the result of his mother's affair with Arch Golden.

Did his father know? Did anyone else? In a community as small as this one, secrets were damned hard to keep. He wanted to keep this one. If he burned the cedar box and the letters could he make this hideous secret go away? Probably not.

The late-night rides his mother had dragged him on to the Pink Palace now made a sick kind of sense. According to the letters, he'd been conceived at the boarding house, and Golden had planned to return for them. His mother had promised to wait for him each month on the anniversary of their meeting.

She claimed to love the actor.

But she also claimed to love her husband.

He scrubbed a hand across his face and tried to understand how a woman could love two men simultaneously. Equally. Differently. He wanted to go down the hall, knock on his father's door and ask him how that was possible. But he wouldn't.

He lifted the last letter again and reread the last paragraphs.

Jack is a good man. He deserves a woman who can love him without being jealous of the land that is such an important part of who he is. There are women in our community who wouldn't mind that he spends more time with his horse than his wife. The best thing I can do is clear the way for him to find that woman.

I'm writing this last letter as I pack to leave. A friend I met at work has offered to drive me to Mexico. He tells me divorces are quick and easy there. I hope that once I'm free you'll still find a place for me and my boys in your heart.

I tried to tell Patrick the truth today, but he wasn't ready to hear it. I will tell him, but I don't want him to hate me. When he's old enough to understand the mistakes I've made, I'll try again, but Arch, my love, until then I beg you to keep our secret.

Patrick swallowed the lump in his throat and dropped the page. He remembered the day she'd tried to tell him about love. He'd thought she'd found out what he'd been doing down by the creek with his girl-friend and he'd been embarrassed. He'd made an excuse and bolted.

Golden had certainly kept her secret, but not long enough.

Rubbing the headache stabbing his temple, he thought about his father, Jack. Jack believed his wife had been running away with her lover when she'd died. Patrick didn't know how he could correct him without reopening an old wound and inflicting more pain.

Along with the letters, Leanna had provided a copy of Golden's will. He pushed the stack of flowered sta-tionery aside and picked up the formal pages from the lawyer's office. He'd skimmed enough to know that his inheritance, though staggering, would do more harm than good if he accepted it. He'd meant it when he told Leanna that it was too late for Arch Golden to make amends.

His birth certificate listed Jack Lander as his father. As far as he was concerned Jack *was* his father. He wouldn't discredit or humiliate him by accepting guilt money from an adulterous stranger.

He'd sign it all over to Leanna and then she could do whatever she wanted with it. If the press showed up he'd tell them they'd been misinformed. Sure, Golden had been a top dog in Hollywood for the past couple of decades, but if he denied the claims, the press would lose interest.

The shower shut off in the bathroom. He dropped the will back into the box and closed the lid. Seconds later a tap on the door preceded Leanna's freshly scrubbed face in the opening.

"Patrick? Are you okay?" The concern in her eyes squeezed his heart.

Hell no, he wasn't okay. He didn't even know who he was. He wasn't Jack Lander's son. He wasn't part of the third generation of Landers to live on Crooked Creek. Where did that leave him? He didn't belong here—had no right to claim a portion of this land.

"I'm fine."

Looking flushed and damp from her shower in her terry cloth robe, she came into the room uninvited and sat on the bed beside him. Her vanilla scent wrapped around him.

Man, he'd love to lose himself inside her right now and forget this damned box and the ticking bomb inside it. Mindless sex was something he understood, something he was comfortable with. The emotion clogging his throat and making him want to pull Leanna close and hold her, on the other hand, was decidedly *un*comfortable.

"I want to help." Hesitantly she reached out and touched his shoulder.

Sparks ignited beneath her fingertips. He shrugged her off. "Well, you can't. Go to bed."

"You need to be with someone who cares about you right now, Patrick. Let me stay."

He closed his eyes and swallowed hard. His stomach knotted like a tight fist, and when he looked into her hazel eyes again, he wished he could be the man she thought he was. But he wasn't. Nobody could be that perfect. He'd only disappoint her if he tried to pretend otherwise.

"I'm not the paragon she described, Leanna. My mother was trying to get Golden to come back for us. She did a major whitewashing of the truth. The man you *think* you know doesn't exist."

She held his gaze. "You're wrong. I've seen him. He cares about his family, and he has unbelievable patience with whiny kids. And just today, I heard him tell a clumsy little girl that she had the makings of a fine cowgirl."

His face burned and he shifted, uneasy with her praise. "You don't need to do this."

A frown puckered her brows. "This?"

"Cozy up to me. We'll see a lawyer tomorrow. I'll sign the entire estate over to you."

"You can't refuse your inheritance. If you do, then it all goes to the list of organizations Arch named. Didn't you see the list?"

He ground his teeth. "I saw it. Every single one of those corporations is against independent ranchers and pro conglomerate beef cattle operations."

A smile tugged up the corners of her lush mouth, but the sadness in her eyes was hard to miss. "Arch wanted to make sure you wouldn't refuse."

"I'm refusing, anyway. I'll find some way around—"

"There are no loopholes. Arch made certain of that. Accept your inheritance, and I'll help you disperse it to causes you believe in—if you insist. I'd rather see you use it to help your family—especially Jack."

That she'd even consider his father thawed a piece of his heart that had frozen when he'd read the letters.

"How will I explain a sudden windfall of fifteen million dollars?"

"I think you're going to have to be honest."

He shook his head and grimaced when his knotted neck muscles protested. He tried to rub out the kinks. "Not this time. What about Golden's lawyer? He used to be Brooke's. Can I trust him to keep his mouth shut?"

"Arch trusted him, but everybody has a price, Patrick. Or so my mother always said." The mattress shifted as she got on her knees behind him. She brushed his hand out of the way.

The gentle kneading of her fingers on his neck didn't ease the ache in his heart. It merely shifted his focus to an ache lower down. The urge to lean back against her and let her distract him from his troubles nearly overpowered him.

Their gazes met in the mirror—the mirror framed by pictures of his brothers. *Half* brothers, he corrected.

"They're your family. They won't let you down."

He wished he shared her confidence. Shoving to his feet, he carried the box to the closet and pushed it to the back of the top shelf. He turned around and found her watching him with that soft, concerned look in her eyes. The warmth invading his chest made him edgy. He tried to ignore it, because he didn't want her to care about him. He'd only hurt her.

"I want to help."

"Go to bed, Leanna." The need to pull her close grew stronger. She knew his dirty secret and she didn't condemn him for being Arch Golden's bastard. He took a step toward her and lifted his hand to brush back her baby-fine hair, but dropped it instead. Touching her would only complicate the situation. "I need to figure out who I am right now."

"Reading the letters didn't change your DNA, Patrick. You're the same person."

"Doesn't feel like it. If I don't tell my family then I'm a liar. If I do, I'm a selfish bastard. I don't want to be either one." And he didn't want to consider the ramifications of the truth getting out. The least that would happen would be that his father would be hurt.

The worst…he'd lose his home, his family.

A no-win situation.

Seven

Patrick's world had been turned upside down, and Leanna felt partially responsible. She wanted to help but didn't know how.

When she'd been frightened, Arch had held her until her fears passed. She moved closer to Patrick, wrapped her arms around his waist and laid her head against his chest.

His muscles went rigid and his heart hammered beneath her cheek. He gripped her shoulders firmly and put a few inches between them.

"Leanna, I'm not strong enough to be smart right now."

She tipped back her head. "This isn't about being smart, Patrick. It's about needing comfort. Arch used to hold me until I fell asleep."

His jaw muscles twitched and then his mouth twisted

into a carnal smile that stole her breath. "If we get into that bed we won't be sleeping."

Her heart tripped and her stomach bottomed out. She was already half in love with him. Did she dare risk falling the rest of the way and going off the deep end the way her mother did if—*when*—their relationship ended?

She'd promised herself that she'd hold out for a hero. Well, she'd found one. What was she going to do about it?

She studied the deep grooves in Patrick's face and knew she couldn't leave him to face his anguish alone. If she paid a price for helping him, then so be it.

She cupped his stubbled cheeks. "I'm here for you."

He closed his eyes tightly and exhaled several shaky breaths. Beneath her fingertips his jaw muscles flexed. His determination to be strong and to get through this alone made her eyes burn.

Standing on tiptoe, she pressed her lips to his. He reared back, but she held fast, kissing him again. Their lips clung, separated, met again and lingered.

Suddenly Patrick banded her with his arms, practically crushing her against his chest.

"Don't regret this," he whispered against her temple.

Gallant even in his time of need. She lifted her head and touched her smile to his chin. "I won't."

As if the words broke through his dam of restraint, he took her mouth, devouring her with an unleashed hunger that left her breathless and dizzy.

His hands skated down to cup her bottom and pull her close. Through her thick bathrobe his heat warmed her, aroused her. He peppered kisses on her mouth, her

chin, her cheek, until he caught her face in his hands.
''Be sure.''

The need in his dark eyes erased any doubts. She'd
never been surer of anything in her life. ''I'm posi-
tive.''

He took a deep breath and straightened. She didn't
understand why he was letting her go until he reached
for the knot of her belt. Patrick plucked at the knot
with unsteady fingers until it gave way, and then he
eased the fabric off her shoulders.

She shrugged and it slid to the floor, leaving her in
her long nightgown. She reached for one of the tiny
bows on her shoulder, but he caught her hand, thread-
ing his fingers through hers and pressed her palm to
his chest.

''Let me.'' He kissed her neck, sipping and sampling
the skin behind her ear until a shiver swept over her.
His evening beard prickled deliciously against her
oversensitized skin, directly contrasting with the softness of his lips, the searing slickness of his tongue.

The nip of his teeth made her gasp. She dug her
fingers into his shoulders and locked her shaky knees.
Heat and tension tangled low in her belly.

He suckled the tendons of her neck, the pulse at the
base of her throat, her earlobe. His hands dipped lower,
stroking over her silky gown to cup her buttocks. Cool
air touched the backs of her calves and thighs as he
eased up the hem, and then his callused palms cupped
her bare bottom. Rough skin and a gentle touch. She
released a shaky breath.

He lifted his head and captured her gaze. The hunger
in his eyes consumed her as he caressed her. Hard.
Soft. Hot. Sensations tumbled through her brain faster
than she could process them. Patrick bent and caught

the ribbon on her shoulder between his teeth and tugged. The bow gave way and the fabric fell to bare her breast.

His chest rose and fell beneath her palms as he inhaled deeply. He dipped his head to brush his lips over her forehead, her nose, her chin, before skating down the opposite side of her neck to the other bow. It too, gave way with the tug of his teeth.

Only Patrick's grip on her waist kept the garment from falling to the floor, and then he lifted his hands and the gown slithered down her legs to land in a puddle at her feet. He stepped back, consuming her with his gaze, and her knees went weak.

The passion in his dark eyes chased away any self-consciousness she might have felt. He liked what he saw. His approval was obvious in his expanding pupils and the rasp of his breath. She'd never felt more beautiful, more desirable in her life.

His gaze never left hers as he undressed. Button after button. Belt. Boots. Socks. Jeans. She savored the slow revelation of bronzed skin. As each item hit the floor it became more difficult to remain passive. She had to open her mouth to breathe, and her nipples tightened almost to the point of pain. She shifted her thighs, trying to ease the emptiness between them. Every inch of her trembled with anticipation.

Clad only in his briefs, Patrick reached for her again, capturing her mouth and her cry when they met skin to skin. She burned with sensation everywhere they touched. From the tease of the wiry hairs on his chest, belly and legs to the stroke of his big hands over her shoulders, spine and hips. He devoured her mouth with long lingering tastes and quick, impatient bites.

The hot, hard press of his erection against her belly

made her achy and impatient. She opened her eyes only to close them again when he captured her breast with his lips. He suckled and plucked one and then the other, teasing and then pulling harder. Slick tongue. Raspy beard. Soft lips. Callused fingers.

She thought she'd go out of her mind. A fire kindled in her belly and a sound pushed itself from her throat.

The soft sweep of his hair on her breast was little warning for the scalding line he blazed with his tongue down her breastbone and across her waist as he knelt before her. He kneaded her bottom, holding her captive while he tasted his way from one hipbone to the other before sampling her navel. She could barely stand still.

His kisses traveled lower, and although she suspected what he'd do next, nothing could prepare her for the shockingly intimate possession of his mouth. Her knees buckled.

Patrick caught her in his arms and stole her breath with a long, slow kiss as she slid to the braided rug beside him. He traced the outline of her lips with his tongue and eased her legs apart with a gentle hand to stroke the slick folds of tender skin. She threw her head back to gasp for breath. He kissed a path of fire across her breasts, her belly, and then he feasted on her.

She dug her nails into the rug and arched her back as pleasure mounted with unbearable swiftness. Just when she thought she'd explode into a million fragments, Patrick pulled away to string kisses along her thigh, her knee, her ankle and back up the opposite leg.

When he reached the heart of her again, she tangled her fingers in his hair, begging without words for him to end her torment. Within seconds he sent her skyward to arch over the room like a shooting star. Panting for breath, she slowly floated back to earth.

But he wasn't satisfied. He sent her soaring again. Her muscles quivered, leaving her too weak to protest when he scooped her up and laid her in the center of his bed. He turned away and her insides clenched with doubt. She sat up, tugging the sheets to cover herself. Was he leaving her? Had she done something wrong?

Patrick stopped in the bathroom, pulled open the cabinet, and extracted a box of condoms. He returned and set the box on the bedside table. "Leanna, now's the time to say no."

As if she could. She'd always expected this moment to be awkward and embarrassing, but it was neither. Kneeling on the bed, she wrapped her arms around his waist, cradling the thick ridge in his briefs between her breasts.

"I want to make love with you, Patrick," she whispered against his skin and then pressed her lips to his beaded nipple. She'd read that men enjoyed it as much as women, and the sharp breath he sucked in proved it to be true. Emboldened by his reaction, she lightly raked her nails down his back and transferred her attention to the opposite side.

He shuddered and groaned, tangled his fingers in her hair and held her close. She cautiously stroked one finger down the fabric barely containing his erection. He jerked at her touch and threw his head back. His jaw and neck muscles strained.

He eased her backwards pressing a quick, hard kiss on her lips before he stood, kicked off his briefs and reached for the condom.

Lying back on the pillows, she held out her arms. Patrick made swift work of the protection and joined her on the bed, aligning his body with hers. The weight of him, the length and heat of him pressed her into the mattress. His muscular thighs parted hers. With the moment of truth arriving, she couldn't help but tense up.

"Easy now." Braced on one arm, he nuzzled her temple and traced her wetness with blunt fingertips, teasing her back to fever pitch. He settled himself over her. His thick tip probed her entrance, and he paused. "You are so wet, so hot."

She twisted beneath his touch, eager, hungry, needy. The stroke of his finger sent her skyward again, and at her peak, he thrust deep. She cried out at the brief flash of pain, but quickly adjusted to the incredible fullness of Patrick seated so deeply inside her she would swear their souls touched.

His trembling muscles shook the bed as he held himself rigid above her. Slowly he opened his eyes, and his dark gaze burned into hers. He bent and brushed a kiss over her lips.

She'd never felt closer to anyone in her life. Wrapping her arms around his waist, she opened for him and he slid deeper.

He groaned against her neck and slowly withdrew, but she didn't want him to go. Curling her hands over his taut bottom, she pulled him back. Again and again he plumbed her depths and withdrew. His pace grew faster, and her own arousal rekindled until she soared.

Patrick bowed his back, thrust harder and then shuddered above her. He collapsed to his elbows and for a few precious moments they were face-to-face, eye to eye, body to body, as intimate as a man and a woman can be, and she knew that this had to be love.

For better or worse, she'd fallen in love with Arch's son.

He rolled to his side, pulling her into the crook of his shoulder and held her close.

Her lids grew heavy. She smiled sleepily and stroked from his chest to his belly. He whistled a breath in through his teeth and caught her wandering fingers. "Leanna—"

She heard the regret in his voice and her heart clenched. She'd have regrets soon enough, but for now she wanted to hold on to her hero. "Shhhh. Sleep. We'll talk tomorrow."

Six miles of uneasy silence stretched inside the truck cab.

Patrick kept his eyes on the road, because the hurt in Leanna's eyes was pretty darned obvious even to a thick-headed jerk like him. He'd left her asleep in his bed this morning. Hell, he'd had to feed the animals and he hadn't wanted his father—he winced—*Jack* to know he'd taken advantage of a guest.

He shouldn't have to tell Leanna how difficult it had been to pry himself out of bed and leave her all warm and flushed between the sheets. A more experienced woman would know it had been incredible between them because he'd reached for her a number of times during the night.

But he hadn't slept with an experienced woman. He'd taken Leanna's virginity. Virgins wanted permanence, and he didn't have it in him. He was genetically encoded to be unfaithful. It was bad enough to know that his mother had cheated, but hell, every tabloid in the country reported on the parade of women through Arch Golden's life.

He tightened his hands on the wheel. He'd have to start damage control, but for now he wanted to savor the fact that Leanna had given him something no one else had ever given him.

She believed in him.

"Patrick, if you don't want to go, we don't have to."

He glanced her way before returning his attention to the road. "You think I'd welsh on a bet?"

"No, but I'd understand if you didn't want to go to the Pink Palace. I can choose another forfeit."

He ground his teeth. How could she be so damned nice? He'd used her. Worse, he wanted to again. He wanted to taste the passion on her lips and see the excitement in her eyes when he taught her new ways to find and give pleasure.

He shifted in his seat, trying to adjust the snug fit of his jeans. "Right. I'm going."

What in the hell had he done? He'd taken a bad situation and made it worse. His world had fallen apart and he'd selfishly used his desire for Leanna to choke his own fears.

No matter how incredible making love with her might have been, it had been wrong. Flat-out stupid.

But he was smart enough to recognize the soft, dreamy look in her eyes. She thought he was a saint. Hell, everybody in the county knew he was damned far from it.

She thought she was in love.

That scared the hell out of him.

He'd loved two women in his life and both had dumped him. His cut-and-run motto saved heartache on both sides, but there was no way he could look into those big hazel eyes and tell her this had been a huge mistake.

"Could we stop by Pete's and see if my car is ready?" She crossed her legs, and the skirt of her dress rode up to reveal a couple more inches of those amazing legs.

"Sure." He struggled to keep his eyes on the road. Another silent mile passed while he tried not to think of how easy it would be to pull off the road and unbutton her dress from neck to hem. Her sandals would be easy to remove and her toe ring… He liked the toe ring.

He caught his leer in the rearview mirror, shook his head and tried to remember what had been brewing in his mind all morning. "This is about my mother's letters, isn't it?"

"What do you mean?"

"You've cooked all my favorites this week."

She shrugged. "I like them, too."

"And the slingshot?"

Her cheeks pinked. "It sounded like a fun hobby when I read about it and something I could do by myself. I didn't have many friends."

His heart contracted, but it wasn't love. It was just sympathy. Her life must've sucked. "You fish?"

"I have, but I don't really like it. I didn't learn all of your hobbies, only the ones that interested me."

"Football?"

"I watch, and of course I cheer for the Dallas Cowboys."

A smile curled his lips. "Damn straight."

"Arch has—"

He held up a hand. "I don't want to talk about Arch."

"You'll have to sooner or later. The press vultures will be all over this."

He hoped she was wrong. He slowed at the entrance to Pete's parking lot and then accelerated past the driveway without stopping. "Pete's not here."

"How can you tell?"

"His car's not here. A '67 Mustang. Sweetest little baby you ever saw. I've been trying to buy that car from Pete since I was thirteen." He glanced at her. "I guess you know about my fixation with the car. It was in my mother's letters."

"I knew." She shifted in her seat. "I need some things from my car. Can we call him on his cell phone?"

"Doesn't have one."

"Does the garage have an alarm?"

He shot her a sharp glance. "No. Why?"

"Because I can pick the lock."

Leanna continued to surprise him. He pulled into the Pink Palace's driveway, killed the engine and turned in his seat. "What's so important you'd break into the garage to get it?"

"I have some of Arch's things that you need to see. I can get inside the building without damaging anything, and I won't touch anything that's not mine."

"I'm not interested in Arch's stuff, and I've done my time with the sheriff. Why do you have this particular job skill?"

"Before Arch took me in I slept in garages or guest houses. The only way to get in was by picking the locks."

He swore. How in the hell could the authorities let a kid live this way? Hadn't anybody cared? Her mother obviously hadn't. His mother might not have been the best, but at least he'd never doubted that she loved him. *Until she'd left.*

No kid of his would ever doubt… Scratch that. He didn't plan to have a wife or kids. Ever.

"It was better than sleeping in a box in an alley." Her tone sounded defensive.

"I'm not angry with you, but I'd like to talk some sense into your mother."

"Good luck. None of the therapists we've hired thus far have managed to keep her straightened out. She's back in rehab now. The second of three months of total lock-down. No communication with the outside world."

He didn't know what to say.

"Let's get this over with." He shoved open his door and circled the truck to open hers. Leanna bounded out of the cab and practically raced up the sidewalk. He followed at a slower pace, his gut knotting tighter with every step. He was almost too tense to admire her shapely calves.

She rang the bell.

Penny answered the door. Her overly made-up eyes shifted from him to Leanna and back. "I don't rent by the hour."

Leanna blushed like only a virg—*near virgin* could. "Ms. Swain? I'm Leanna Jensen. You probably already know Patrick Lander. I've come to check out your ghost."

"Well, come on in, then."

He took a deep breath and followed. He hadn't been inside the Palace since he was a kid. The madam's portrait still hung over the desk in the foyer. Her gaze had always seemed to follow him and still did. It gave him the creeps then and now, especially when he realized the madam's eyes were the same greeny gold as Leanna's.

Penny stepped behind the desk. "I'll give you a couple of hours to roust Annabel, but I can't guarantee she'll appear."

Leanna grinned. "That's half the fun. Arch and I always loved the waiting part."

"Arch?" Penny's gaze darted toward him. She shifted on her heels and tangled her fingers.

"Arch Golden was my employer up until his death. We investigated a lot of ghost sightings."

Patrick noticed the trembling of Penny's hands when she patted her dyed red hair and the flush creeping up her neck and into her hairline.

He couldn't wait. "Golden met my mother here."

Penny's eyes rounded in horror, and her color faded. "I...don't remember. It's been so long."

"I'll bet you do."

Penny twitched under his stare. "It's not like you think."

"Then tell me how it is."

Leanna laid a hand on his arm. "Patrick—"

"Call me a fool, but I want to understand how my mother could deliberately destroy our family."

Penny sighed and her shoulders sagged. "You'd better come into the parlor."

Leanna's fingers curled around his. Patrick fought the urge to squeeze her hand and hold on tight, but needing her like this made him feel weak. Pulling free, he followed the women into the parlor.

His mother had probably spent time in this room. With Golden. Bile burned his throat.

He couldn't sit. He needed to pace. Hell, he needed a horse and a long, fast ride to clear his head. Better yet, a shot of tequila. Maybe a full bottle.

He stopped by the mantel and clenched his fists. "Tell me what you know about my mother and Golden."

Penny fidgeted. "Would you like tea or—"

"No." She flinched at his harsh tone, and he added, "Thanks."

She perched on the edge of a chair, looking decidedly ill-at-ease. "You knew your mother and Jack weren't a love match, didn't you?"

He hadn't known until last year when his father had made the surprising confession to Brand. His parents' marriage had come after an accidental pregnancy. "Yeah."

"Carolyn came from a wealthy family in Dallas. When they found out she was pregnant, her parents kicked her out. She called Jack for help, and Jack, being an old-fashioned son of a gun, married her even though we—" She bit her lip.

"The marriage started off rocky, but Carolyn began to care for Jack. She needed reassurance that he returned her feelings, but…I don't have to tell you that he's not the demonstrative sort."

"No." His father had always been short on praise and long on criticism.

"Arch, on the other hand, was a charmer. He knew how to make a gal feel special. Half the women in town were chasing him, but he was only interested in the one who wasn't. Your mother."

"Yeah, right. She was so uninterested she slept with him."

Penny ignored his sarcasm. "Carolyn was a misfit, like me, and we were friends. She resisted Arch until she got this wild idea that seeing him might make Jack jealous. She didn't plan for it to go as far as it did, and she didn't plan on falling in love. I don't think Arch did either."

His chest tightened until it hurt to breathe. He swallowed, but the knot in his throat didn't budge. He hardened his heart. His mother had committed adultery, which in his mind was unforgivable.

"She found herself torn between Arch and Jack. Jack provided the stability and security she needed, but Arch gave her the attention and excitement your father didn't.

"It didn't last long, only a couple of months, before Jack found out. He busted up Arch pretty good and put him on a bus to California. I didn't hear from Arch again until he got a small part in a movie."

"You kept in touch?"

She popped up. "I'm parched. I think I'll make coffee."

He blocked the door. "Did you keep in touch with Golden?"

"Yes." She seemed reluctant to offer the information. "Mostly though your mother, but sometimes he wrote me to see how she was doing."

"Did he ask about me?"

Her gaze darted away from his and the hair on the back of his neck rose. She wrung her hands. "After your mother died he'd call and I'd tell him what I knew."

He sucked a sharp breath. "You spied on me?"

She stiffened, parking her hands on her ample hips. "Somebody had to or Arch would have been on the first plane back. We wouldn't have wanted that to happen, now would we?"

Hell, no. "Who else knows?"

"About Carolyn and Arch?"

His neck muscles protested when he nodded. Leanna looped her arm through his. He needed her support too much to shake her off. He'd worry about that later.

"Other than Jack, probably nobody. Carolyn was my

friend. Folks wouldn't think twice about her coming to visit me."

"Who knows about me?"

She didn't pretend not to understand what he meant. "I didn't tell anybody, but you look just like him, Patrick. You Lander men are all good-looking, but *you,* you're Hollywood handsome.

"One thing you need to remember, Patrick, is that your momma stayed with Jack for eighteen years. She tried to make it work, but she was miserable. She worried about how that was affecting you boys. You'd started getting into all kinds of trouble. Caleb's grades were falling. Brand was only eight years old and already getting into fights at school, and Cort was the most miserable baby in the county. She honestly believed that divorcing Jack would be for the best, for everybody."

His mother's letters said as much, but he couldn't understand how tearing a family apart could ever benefit anyone. He rubbed the back of his neck and tried to make sense of this convoluted mess.

Leanna squeezed his arm. "Could you show us the room now, Ms. Swain?"

"Sure thing, honey. I'm guessing you two would like some time alone."

He followed Penny and Leanna up the wide, curving stairs to a long landing. Dread pulled at his feet. He'd had nightmares about this house. He rubbed the ache in his chest. "Which room did they use?"

Penny stopped in front of a door with a brass number ten on it. "Room ten. Arch had a thing about ghosts even then."

Eight

Leanna squeezed between Patrick and the door of room ten. "Let's go home."

Patrick set his jaw and squared his shoulders. His mother had cheated on his father here. This was one ghost he had to face. "No."

Her somber eyes pleaded with him. "Please, Patrick, you don't have to do this. I cancel the bet."

He looked over Leanna's head to Penny. "Unlock the door."

Penny used a skeleton key in the old brass lock, turned the knob and pushed the door open. She pressed the key into his hand. "Remember, son, it takes two to make a relationship work. It also takes two to break one."

She left them and went back down the stairs.

He forced his legs forward, entered the room and stopped in surprise. He'd expected the room to look like a whore house, but it looked like any other bedroom.

He didn't want to feel sympathy for his mother or to shift any part of the blame for the disintegration of their marriage to his father—to Jack. He sure as hell didn't want to accept any part of the blame, but according to Penny, his high jinks had contributed to his mother's desertion.

"Patrick, let's go." The sympathy and understanding in Leanna's eyes made his throat clog.

"You wanted your ghost. I don't welsh on bets." He pulled her into his arms and kissed her a little harder than he should. He didn't want to think about this room or what had happened here. Losing himself in Leanna seemed like the best solution.

Instead of slapping him the way she should have for his rough treatment, she wrapped her arms around his waist and held tight, offering comfort he realized he sorely needed. He eased up, soothing her bruised lips with butterfly kisses.

The tang of salt on his tongue made him draw back. Tear trails streaked her cheek. He was a jerk. "Don't cry."

"I didn't drag you here to hurt you."

Her concern melted his heart like saddle soap left in the sun. He pulled her forward, tucking her head beneath his chin, and inhaled the sunshine scent of her hair. She felt good in his arms, but that didn't mean she belonged there.

With a sigh of resignation, he eased a few inches between them. "I'm not the man for you."

She tipped her head back and met his gaze. "Why not?"

"Because you're in love with the character my

mother created. That's not me. Hell, my father—
Jack—was on a first-name basis with all of my teachers
and most of the county's law enforcement officers. You
heard Penny. I stayed in trouble.''

"What kind of trouble?"

"Mostly skipping school. A little car racing. A lot
of underage drinking.''

Her hand was soft on his cheek, her thumb, an erotic
caress on his lips. "Sounds like most of the teens
where I come from.''

Most of the teens, but not her. "I'll bet you were
too busy trying to survive to ever raise any hell. I'm
not good enough for you, Leanna.''

She stepped back and paced toward a chair in the
corner. She turned, arms folded, chin thrust forward.
"Did you ever steal anything?''

"No."

"Well, I did. Twice while I lived on the streets, I
stole food, and once when I was so sick I could barely
breathe I went through the pharmacy's dumpster and
stole a bottle of antibiotics.''

From her wary, defensive expression, he gathered
she expected him to hate her for stealing to stay alive.
He couldn't. "And I'll bet as soon as you had the
money you paid 'em back.''

She blushed. "Of course, but that's not the point.''

His anger at her mother for putting Leanna in such
a dangerous situation battled with fear for what could
have happened. He watched the news enough to know
that most teenage girls who ran away ended up as
hookers, on drugs or dead. And never having the
chance to know Leanna Jensen was something he
didn't want to contemplate.

In two strides he stood beside her. He should probably resist the urge to kiss her, but he couldn't. He wanted to forget the lie his life had been and the disaster hers had been.

The touch of her soft lips on his inflamed him. They were both breathing hard by the time a speck of common sense encroached on his pleasure. He lifted his head. "This isn't a good idea."

"Didn't you like making love with me?" The doubts in her eyes ripped through his heart like barbed wire.

He stroked her soft cheek. "You know I did. I went off like a Roman candle every time, angel, but our relationship can't go anywhere. You're the forever type and I'm…not."

A frown puckered her brow. "I didn't ask for forever."

Not in words, but her need to be loved was so obvious a blind man could see it. Damned if he didn't wish he could be the man she needed. But he couldn't, and he couldn't bear to see the disappointment in her eyes when she figured that out. "You want to find your ghost?"

"Maybe later. Right now I need you to hold me, and I think you need me, too."

He couldn't deny it.

He sat down in the chair and pulled her across his lap, draping her legs over the arm.

She twined her arm around his neck and burrowed against him like she couldn't get close enough. Her other hand kindled a path of fire across his chest. His blood took a turn south.

He groaned when she shifted and her bottom ground against his erection. "Leanna—"

Her breath warmed his neck and his heart raced faster than it had his very first time. He'd bet she had no idea that she was driving him right out of his mind when he felt the tentative touch of her lips on his jaw.

Lifting her chin with his knuckle, he dipped his head and sipped from her lips. Her fingers flexed like a kitten's on his chest, on his nape, and she made a hungry noise deep in her throat.

He lifted his head enough to look into her eyes. "You know where this is headed, don't you?"

A slow smile curved her lips and a blush coated her cheeks. "I know."

The woman had a siren's smile and an angel's heart. Heaven help him, he didn't want to break it.

He dragged his fingers down her spine to the spot he'd learned made her shiver and back up again to her nape. He took her mouth, pouring all the confusing emotions she stirred up in him into his kiss. He worked the buttons of her dress with his free hand, not ending his quest until he'd unhooked her front-clasp bra and cupped bare, warm flesh in his palm.

Her nipple pebbled beneath the scrape of his thumbnail. He teased it until she whimpered, and then bent to taste her. Her vanilla scent filled his senses as he suckled. She squirmed in his lap, tormenting him as she ground against him. He made quick work of the remaining buttons and pushed the sides of her dress apart.

She lay, nearly bare, in his lap. Pale pink flushed her cheeks, her breasts. Her panties were damp. Leanna was so damned responsive. He smiled into her slumberous, sexy eyes and brushed his thumb over the silky fabric until she gasped. "Like that?"

"Mmmm."

"How 'bout this?" He eased his fingers beneath the elastic and into her curls. She arched into his touch and moaned as he stroked her to satisfaction. He caught the sound with his mouth and then quickly stripped her panties down her legs. She kicked them free. Her sandals hit the floor with the bang of a starting gun, and his heart sprinted.

Her short nails scraped his skin as her nimble fingers attacked the buttons of his shirt. He sucked in a swift breath and shuddered. Much more of that and he'd blow.

He chuckled. Maybe she knew what she was doing, after all.

Lifting her in his arms, he stood to survey the room. He wanted her, but *not in that bed*. The thick rug on the floor in front of the fire would do. In two strides he lowered her onto it. Her dress spread around her and her silky hair haloed her face. Warm. Wet. Willing. And wanting him. What had he ever done in his misspent life to deserve such a treat?

In ten seconds he'd stripped off his clothes, pausing only to retrieve a condom from his pocket. He knelt beside her and she smiled. The trust in her eyes gripped him, squeezing his heart and his throat.

Oh, hell. He was falling for her.

He closed his eyes against the fear—fear of falling, fear of *failing*—and aligned his body with hers. Her calves met behind his back, reeling him into her heat, and he was a goner. He couldn't ride fast enough, plunge deep enough or get enough of her mouth. Her whimpers tasted better than anything he'd ever experienced, and her wiggles nearly unmanned him. The contracting of her inner muscles pulled him over the edge.

Too soon. Too intense. So damned perfect he was afraid to open his eyes and find out he was dreaming.

He forced his lids open anyway, ready to face the cold hard facts.

She stroked his cheek and that siren's smile curved her damp, swollen lips.

A cold breeze brushed over his back causing goose bumps, and for a moment he thought he smelled another woman's perfume, but then Leanna pulled him close and his mind cleared of anything except the press of her silky skin against him. He rolled on his side and held her close. Warmth covered him like a flannel blanket.

Lying in her arms felt good, right. He'd always been a gambler, and the odds weren't good, but maybe he should take a chance on love working out for him.

"I guess Penny's wondering what we're doing." The husky whisper of her voice turned him on almost as much as the fingers she wove through his chest hair.

"Probably, and if you don't stop that she's liable to walk in and find us doing it again."

"Not up to the challenge, cowboy?"

Her husky chuckle was one-hundred-proof aphrodisiac. It went straight to his head...and elsewhere. He had to kiss that sassy smile off her lips.

A crowd surrounded the ambulance parked in the Landers' driveway.

Leanna's heart sank. She'd recognize those intrusive, camera-toting vultures anywhere.

"What in the hell?" Patrick muttered. He floored the engine up the remaining stretch of driveway and brought the truck to a skidding halt in the gravel beside the crowd.

"Paparazzi." She spat the word like a curse.

His gaze pinned her. "You expected them?"

"Not *today*." She should have had another week to convince Patrick to talk to Jack.

"Somebody's hurt." He opened the door to the truck and the reporters surrounded him like a pack of hungry wolves. Cameras clicked and whirred.

One man shoved a microphone in his face. "Patrick Lander?"

"Yeah."

The reporter continued, "I'm with the *L.A. News*, Mr. Lander. Is it true that you're Arch Golden's son and heir?"

Patrick sliced a hard look her way.

Leanna shook her head. "We have no comment at this time."

She hated to abandon him, but she needed to know who was in that ambulance. "Just keep saying no comment. I'm going to see who's hurt."

She climbed from the truck and cut her way through the crowd to the vehicle. Fear tightened her chest and dread weighted her steps. Her chest was so tight she could barely breathe by the time she'd elbowed her way through the crowd. Her worst fears were confirmed.

Jack. He lay on the stretcher in the back of the ambulance. His face was pasty and sweaty and his eyes were closed. His shirt had been removed and wires ran from his chest to a monitor inside the vehicle. An IV had been attached to one hand.

"Is he okay?"

The paramedic turned her way. "Are you the next of kin?"

"No, but his son is here." Leanna stood on the bumper of the vehicle and yelled over the babbling reporters. "Patrick! It's Jack."

The color drained from Patrick's face. Leanna didn't wait to watch him fight his way through the reporters. She climbed into the ambulance. "Jack, Patrick's coming."

Jack's eyelids fluttered and his lips moved, but he didn't make a sound.

She squeezed his hand. "We'll take care of you, Jack. Just hang on."

Leanna climbed out of the vehicle and pulled Patrick forward. The fear in his eyes tore her heart. "Ride with them. I'll call your brothers and meet you at the hospital. Take care of Jack. I'll handle the press."

"What happened?" Patrick's voice sounded strangled.

The paramedic said, "We suspect a heart attack. We need to get him to the hospital. The one in Freer is the closest."

"Mr. Lander," one of the camera carrying men called. "Are you Arch Golden's heir?"

"Don't answer." Leanna pushed him into the ambulance. "Go. I'll handle it."

The driver shut the ambulance doors, and Leanna said a silent prayer for Jack. Patrick needed him now more than ever. Surely fate wouldn't be so cruel as to take both of his fathers in the same month.

She climbed the porch steps, faced the vultures and waited until the sound of the sirens faded in the distance before raising a hand to get their attention.

"I'm Leanna Jensen. We have no comment to make at this time, but if you'll leave me your cards, I'll contact you when we have a statement."

A barrage of questions hit her. She shook her head and held up her hands. "I ask that you respect the Landers' privacy in this time of crisis."

* * *

The hospital was cold. Or maybe it was just him.

Patrick paced the waiting room outside the coronary care unit. He'd never been so scared in all his life— not even when he'd been a teenager wondering if the rattlesnake bite he'd sustained would kill him before he could get home.

The waiting room door opened and Brand hustled in. "Where is he? What happened?"

"The doctors think he had a heart attack. They're running tests to determine the extent of the damage." He glanced at his watch. It seemed like days had passed, but it had only been a few of hours.

"What brought it on?"

"An ambush by the press."

"Reporters? What would they want from Dad?" Brand demanded.

"It's not him they want. It's me." His muscles tightened further. "I'm not your brother."

"Huh?"

"Mom had an affair with Arch Golden. I'm…Arch's son."

"Don't be a smart-ass. Now's not the time to crack jokes."

Patrick held his gaze until Brand swore.

"Leanna just told me."

"She's the one who called me?"

"Yeah. She worked for Arch and now she's handling his estate."

Brand's brows shot up. "He left you something?"

"Yeah, but I'm turning it down. I didn't want Dad— *Jack*…" He scrubbed a hand across his face. "Hell, I didn't want any of you to find out, but the reporters were circling that ambulance like vultures."

"Who tipped off the press?"

Who indeed? Only a handful of people knew, and Leanna had expected them.

The waiting room door opened again and Leanna hurried in with Toby hot on her heels. "How is he?"

His throat closed up. Had she called the press? She'd said that she would once the will was filed.

Brand answered. "We don't know yet."

"You must be Brand. I'm Leanna." She turned her hazel eyes on him and Patrick wondered if they were lying eyes. "Cort and Caleb will be here as soon as they can get flights."

Had she been plotting a press conference while making love with him? Hell, for all he knew, she could have planned the outing to the Palace a week ago when she'd wagered that kiss.

The doctor, a man about his own age, came in. "We've administered t-PA, that's a drug used to dissolve clots, and we've made Mr. Lander as comfortable as possible with a morphine drip. Your father has a partially blocked artery. We can keep him here and start him on a regimen of medicines, which can improve the situation, but for a better prognosis I'd recommend emergency angioplasty to reopen the blocked artery. We're not equipped to do that here."

"Then, where?" Leanna calmly asked, when neither Patrick nor Brand spoke up.

"We can Life Flight him to San Antonio, but you need to understand that's an expensive option. I notice that like most ranchers in the region, Mr. Lander doesn't carry health insurance."

Leanna said, "Money's not an issue."

The doctor said, "Are you his daughter?"

She shifted on her feet. Guilty conscience? "No."

"I see." He turned his attention back to Patrick and

Brand. "We need to make a decision quickly. The first hours after onset are the most critical. I can call ahead and have a surgical team waiting."

Patrick rubbed the knotted muscles in the back of his neck. Brand had just tied up a hunk of his money in building a veterinary clinic for his wife. Caleb's money was tied up in the dude ranch, and Cort had just started medical school. That left it to him to raise the money. Mortgaging the ranch wasn't an option.

Leanna laid a hand on his arm. "Money isn't an issue, Patrick. Just say yes."

If he took the money he could lose his family, his home. If he didn't he could lose his father. Maybe he'd lost him already if the reporters had sprung the sordid truth before Jack crashed. He swallowed hard and took a deep breath. "Let's do it."

The doctor nodded and closed the chart. "Good. I'll make the arrangements." He gave them the name of a hospital and a surgeon and left.

Leanna squeezed his arm. "I'll take care of the arrangements on my end. The money will be available whenever you need it. We already have an interested buyer for Arch's mansion. If you want to sell it, all you have to do is say so and the lawyer can start the paperwork."

Her cool, competent attitude and gentle smile hardened his heart. Had she slept with him to force his hand? "Liquidate everything."

"But—"

Was he a magnet for lying women? "Just do it. You've gotten what you wanted. Now get the hell out of my life."

She gasped and staggered back a step. The color

drained from her face. "Patrick, I didn't call the press."

"Right. Be out of the house before I get home."

"I lov—"

He sliced a hand through the air to cut her off. "I wouldn't believe anything you said right now, so save your breath."

He yanked out his wallet and counted out the five hundred dollars he'd been saving to overhaul the tractor's engine. "This should cover what the Double C owes you."

She didn't take the money. Her lips quivered and her eyes filled with tears. He had to give her credit for picking up top-notch acting skills while living with Golden.

"You don't owe me that much."

He took her hand, shoved the money into it and closed her fingers around the bills. "Consider it severance pay. Now get the hell out of here."

She mashed her lips together, nodded and backed out of the waiting room.

Toby glared at him and followed her out.

Brand laid a hand on his shoulder. "You could be wrong."

"Nope. As executrix of Arch's estate she gets two hundred and fifty thousand dollars as soon as everything's settled. Sleeping with me was just a means to hurry me along."

Brand swore. "The Lander curse strikes again."

"Yeah." He'd been cursed all right. Cursed to fall in love with a woman whose only interest was in his bank balance.

Outside the hospital Leanna took a steadying breath. Every man she'd ever cared for had left her, so why did Patrick's rejection hurt so much? She'd known it was coming.

The only question was, would she go off the deep end like her mother? Would she crave alcohol or drugs to anesthetize the pain? Right now, she only craved Patrick—even if she did want to kick him in the shins for believing she would ever deliberately hurt him or Jack.

She turned toward Toby. "Thanks for the ride."

"I'll take you back to the ranch."

"I really need to find Pete and pick up my car."

"You got it. I know where he fishes."

She followed him to the truck. As soon as she got to a pay phone she'd call the lawyer and put the wheels in motion to transfer the money, but she wasn't leaving Texas until Jack was out of danger. No matter what Patrick said.

Toby nervously jangled his keys as they crossed the hospital parking lot. "Saturday's gonna be hellacious."

"What do you mean?"

"Dudes coming in. Maria's still out. Without you or Patrick it'll be rough. He did fire you in there, didn't he?"

"Maybe, but I won't leave you to juggle it all by yourself."

Toby looked doubtful.

"I'll take full responsibility if the Landers get angry."

He shrugged. "Not sure it's a good idea, but I'd appreciate it. Double C's booked solid. Where will you stay?"

Not at the Lander house. Patrick's money sat like a

brick in her pocket, but it wasn't hers. She wouldn't spend it. Storage building, here I come.

"Don't worry, I know of a place."

Patrick awoke with a start. Every muscle in his body protested a long night in a short recliner.

His gaze jerked to the bed. His father still slept. The machines were on and operational.

"Mr. Lander?" The nurse's tone implied she'd called him more than once. She held a good-size box. "This is for you."

He took the package and the scissors she passed him from her pocket. Who would send him a package at the hospital? He split the packaging tape, opened the flaps, and found his duffel bag inside the box. The house key he'd given Leanna dangled from a pale yellow hair ribbon tied to the handle.

He blamed the emptiness in his gut on hunger. Other than vending machine fare, he hadn't eaten since breakfast, yesterday. He didn't miss her, dammit. She'd betrayed him.

He unzipped the bag and found his shaving kit, along with several changes of clothing, some of his favorite beef jerky and a round tin. He pried off the lid. The smell of the fresh-baked cookies made his mouth water. Chocolate chip and oatmeal raisin. His favorites.

"Someone overnighted a care package? How thoughtful."

"Yeah." Why would she, now that she had what she wanted? A farewell gift? Guilty conscience? By now she was probably halfway back to California.

The nurse checked Jack's vitals and wrote in the chart. "The doctor will be in soon." She left.

Patrick heard a groan. Jack's eyes opened. Patrick rushed to the bedside. "Dad?"

"Get me out of here." Jack's voice was a raspy whisper.

Patrick grabbed the cup of ice water the nurse had left and put the straw to his father's mouth. "Let the doctors do their job."

"If it's my time, then I plan on going before you mortgage the ranch."

"That won't happen."

"Can't afford to stay."

Tension knotted his muscles. "Yeah, you can."

"I...know how much...we got in the bank." Jack grimaced.

"It's taken care of."

His father's pain-filled gaze locked with his, but Patrick couldn't find the words to explain how they could suddenly afford an astronomical hospital bill. According to the billing lady, the cost for this room per day was more money than the ranch cleared in a year and Jack would be in intensive care a minimum of three days.

The doctor's entrance gave him a temporary reprieve. "Mr. Lander, you were very lucky."

"Don't feel like it."

"There is very little damage to your heart muscle. We've removed a blockage from your artery. Now you're going to change your ways. You'll reduce your stress levels, take your meds and exercise, so that I don't have to see you here again. A therapist will teach you meditation and biofeedback to help with the pain."

"Mumbo-jumbo."

The doc just shook his head. "Very effective medicine."

The doctor lectured on, but Patrick's mind wandered. They'd had a near miss. How could he explain about Arch and his mother and not risk a repeat?

If Jack didn't bring up the reporters, then maybe they hadn't spilled their story, and he wouldn't until he damned well had to.

Leanna waited outside the hospital until Patrick and his brothers left.

Patrick looked strained and exhausted, and her heart ached for him. Tucking her purse under her arm, she took a deep breath and strode forward. She knew Jack's room number because she'd called earlier and asked.

The hospital smell hit her, reminding her of her final days with Arch and making her throat tighten. In the end Arch had asked to be taken home. He'd sworn there was no fun in haunting a hospital. A sad smile tugged her lips.

She made it past the reception desk in the lobby and into the elevator without incident. She hit the first road-block at the nurses' station on Jack's floor. "Can I help you?"

"I'm here to see Jack Lander." She tried to sound as if she had every right to be there.

"Are you family? Only family is allowed in the CCU."

Think fast. "I'm his daughter-in-law."

"He's with the therapist right now, but you should be able to go in."

She could hear Jack grousing from the hallway as she approached the door. "Ain't learning that mumbo-jumbo."

"Biofeedback," the nurse supplied. "For pain management."

"Call my sons. I wanna go home."

The door opened and a harassed-looking woman stepped out. "I'm not getting anywhere with him."

Leanna looked over the woman's shoulder. Jack lay in bed, his face contorted in pain. "Could I try? I worked with a terminal cancer patient. Toward the end, mind-body medicine is the only thing that worked for him."

"Be my guest, honey." She sounded happy to pass off a difficult patient.

Leanna entered the room with the charge nurse hot on her heels. "Mr. Lander, your daughter-in-law is here to see you."

Leanna waited for Jack to blow her cover, but he didn't. The nurse left them. "Sit down. Quit hovering."

She smiled. "You must be better if you're giving the nurses a hard time."

"You got something you need to tell me?"

She shrugged. "I lied to get in here. I'll leave if you want me to, but first I want to make sure you're okay and to see if you need anything."

"I wanna go home."

She sat down in the chair beside the bed and took his hand in hers. "Jack, Patrick needs you right now more than he's ever needed you before. Please stay and let the doctors help you."

The grooves in his face deepened.

"I'm sorry you found out the way you did. I never meant to hurt you."

"Wasn't news. I knew."

And still he'd loved Carolyn. Her eyes stung.

"As soon as you said you'd worked for Golden, I

knew why you'd come. Even dead, he wanted to take my son.''

"No, Jack, he wants to make amends to Patrick for not ever contributing to his life.''

She dug into her purse and pulled out the photos, the one of Carolyn from his bedroom and the other of the Lander brothers from Patrick's. "Do you want me to put these on your tray table?''

His eyes filled with tears. He mashed his lips and nodded. The machines beside the bed showed an increased heart rate.

"The therapist says you're not interested in biofeedback. Did she explain that all it involves is thinking about your favorite places and people?''

"Said I had to visualize a happy place.'' He said it the same way he'd say she suggested he jump off a bridge.

"Or a happy time in your life, or the people who made you the happiest. Tell me about your favorite place on the ranch.''

After a silent moment, Jack nodded. "There's a grove behind the stock pond. Used to drive there when things got tough or when Carolyn and I needed some time alone. The boys were always underfoot...''

Leanna listened as Jack painted a picture of the stable life she'd always yearned for. Home. Family. Love. The numbers on the monitor dropped down to a safer level.

His voice trailed off, and then after several moments he said, "I wasn't man enough to hold her.''

Leanna covered his hand with hers. "You're wrong. Carolyn loved you very much.''

"Right.''

The sarcastic word sounded so much like Patrick she

bit her lip to stem the tears. "I read the letters she wrote to Arch, and believe me, she loved you."

"Fine way to show it."

"She said you were Matt Dillon to her Miss Kitty. She always knew that when she needed you you'd come running. But she also knew that you'd saddle up and leave her."

"Ranching was my job."

"She knew that, but it didn't keep her from being jealous of your horse, because in her words, the nag spent each and every hour of the day with you." She squeezed his hand and smiled. "She must have loved you a lot to want to be with you all day, every day."

"Then why'd she hook up with Golden?"

"Penny says she did it to make you jealous. Carolyn's letters tell me it's because she needed constant reassurance that she was special. That was her problem, not yours, Jack. Some women are like that. My mother certainly is. If a man's not fawning all over her, she thinks something's wrong."

His eyes fell to half-mast. "Shouldn't need hearts and flowers every danged day. I busted my butt to make enough money to buy her whatever she wanted. Should've been enough."

"Yes, it should have. She was very lucky to have you, Jack."

"Come back tomorrow. Bring the letters." He fell asleep.

Nine

Leanna hid herself in the shadow of the barn until the pickup truck pulled away from the Lander home with Patrick behind the wheel.

The glare of the rising sun on the windshield made it difficult to be sure, but she thought all the Lander sons were inside the cab.

After spending half of her second night with Jack, she'd overslept this morning. Using the horse wash stall was out of the question in daylight. She had to shower and get back to the dude ranch before the rest of the staff arrived at lunchtime. The redecorators had already arrived, so borrowing Brooke's shower was out of the question.

She shifted the package under her arm and pulled her utility tool out of her pocket. With two quick twists, the lock gave way. After a quick check over her shoulder, she let herself inside the kitchen.

First stop, Patrick's room. She set the gift and card Arch had bought for Patrick's thirteenth birthday on the bed, and then jumped into the shower. When she got out she dressed, trying to ignore the circles under her eyes from too little sleep, gathered the clothes from the hamper and headed back downstairs.

She raided the pantry and the freezer and threw together several casseroles. While they cooked she cleaned and dusted the downstairs and folded laundry. When the timer sounded, she headed back to the kitchen, pulled the pecan pie out of the oven and set the hot pan on the stovetop.

The stairs creaked. The hair on the back of neck rose. She spun around.

A man about her age stood on the bottom step. From what Jack had said when describing the Lander boys in the picture she'd taken him, she guessed this had to be Cort Lander. He was handsome and sleep rumpled, but nowhere near as sexy as his brother.

What could she do except brazen her way through this? "Good morning. I've made a couple of casseroles and started on the laundry. I'll be out of your way in a few minutes."

"You're Leanna."

"Yes." She expected him to tell her to get out.

"I'm Cort." He offered his hand and gave hers a brisk shake. "Patrick thinks you're in California."

"I'm not leaving until I'm sure Jack's okay. Besides, I promised Brooke I'd fill in for her until her book tour's finished. I have a contract."

A slow grin curved his lips. "Is that right? Does Patrick know? Of course he doesn't." He chuckled. "You're the one who took the pictures to Dad."

He didn't seem to be angry that she'd visited Jack. "Yes, but how did you know?"

"I stopped by the hospital for a couple of hours early this morning after my plane landed." He approached the pie and sniffed. "Chocolate chip pecan?"

She handed him a knife and a plate. He dug in.

"The nurse says a woman came in last night to help Dad through the worst of the pain. Was that you?" he asked between bites.

"Yes."

He grabbed a pad of paper and wrote a number on it. "They're moving him out of intensive care today. Patrick's with him this morning, but he'll be back at the dude ranch before the dudes come in this afternoon. Here's Dad's new room number." He set his plate in the sink. "Thanks for the pie. I've got to take a shower and get back to the hospital."

He paused on the bottom step. "Leanna, if the nurses on the new floor give you any trouble tonight, just tell them to call me. I'll vouch for you."

Patrick looked across the patio at the dude ranch welcome party and stopped in his tracks.

Anger quickly obliterated the pleasure of seeing Leanna. Why was she here? She'd betrayed him, lied to him, *slept with him,* for crying out loud, and yet there she was, in uniform, laughing and chatting with guests as if he hadn't fired her.

He cut his way across the patio. Toby snagged him. "Did I tell you the pinto looks lame? Maybe you could take a look?"

"Call the vet." He shook free, but only made it a couple of yards before Jan, Maria's assistant, intercepted him.

"Wilbur has a sore throat. You need to see if you can line up another band for tonight's opening shindig."

"You have the list. Start dialing." His gaze tracked Leanna.

She smiled and chatted with a group of kids. He knew the exact second when she became aware of him. Her spine stiffened, and she slowly turned his way.

His breath hitched. She looked like hell. He could see the dark circles under her eyes from thirty feet away. A vise tightened on his heart, but he tamped down any tender feelings. She'd lied to him, used him and almost killed Jack, dammit.

"Jan, call your brother and tell him it's his lucky day. Put his band onstage tonight." He strode forward, his gaze locked with Leanna's.

He nearly collided with Warren and his temper flared. "What is it, Warren?"

"I wanted to ask if I could lead the trail ride tomorrow morning. Or maybe you'll let me take 'em skeet shooting?"

He glared at the ranch hand and then it hit him. They were protecting Leanna. She'd worked her sorcery on the crew the same way she'd hoodwinked him. "Will you get the hell out of my way if I say yes?"

"Ah, um, well, how about—"

"Warren, if you want to keep your job, you'll move. Now."

Warren stepped aside.

Leanna watched him warily, chewing her bottom lip as he stalked her. She worked up a smile, but it didn't reach her wary eyes. "Hi."

"Excuse us," he said to the dude. Cupping Leanna's

elbow, he half led, half dragged her to the edge of the patio. "What are you doing here?"

"My job."

"I fired you."

"Really?"

She folded her arms, drawing his attention to the fabric pulled taut across her sensitive breasts. Hell. His brain had been stuck in his shorts since he'd first laid eyes on her.

"I have a contract with Brooke and Caleb. It says you're required to have just cause to dismiss me *and* you have to give me notice in writing."

He growled in frustration. Brooke and her damned convoluted contracts. She'd even made *him* sign one. "I'll get it."

She tipped up her chin. "If you try, I'll slap you with a sexual harassment suit."

She was bluffing. She had to be. Or did she? The stubborn set to her jaw and the glint in her eyes warned him not to test her. No doubt about it, Leanna was a fighter and he was too danged peeved with her to admire that.

She continued, "And if you fire me, then Brooke will have to come back home. Think of how much money she'll lose if she cancels all her *contracted* public appearances, not to mention the amount of stress you'd be putting her under. Expectant mothers should avoid stress."

She played the guilt card like a professional blackjack dealer. "Keep out of trouble and stay out of my way."

Leanna clicked her heels, saluted and hit him with a downright sassy smile. "You're the boss."

Didn't feel like it. He ground his teeth and shoved

his hands in his pockets to keep from stroking the purple crescents beneath her eyes. "You look like hell."

She wrinkled her nose. "Why, thank you. You look like you could use a few more hours' sleep yourself."

"Where are you staying?"

"I think we had this conversation last week. Can I get back to work? The boss is in a bad mood." She smiled.

He scowled. "Quit pushing my buttons and answer the question."

Her steady gaze held his. "You already know the answer, Patrick."

He swore. He couldn't let her sleep in the shed or get naked in the horse wash stall. It wasn't safe. Back to square one, but dammit, he didn't want a traitor in his house—not to mention the fact that Cort was back in his own room, and because the painters weren't finished at the ranch, Brooke and Caleb were in Caleb's old room. Where would he put her?

Looked like he'd be bunking on the sofa. He wouldn't sleep a wink knowing she was in his bed.

She tucked her hair behind her ears. "Did you get it?"

"Get what?"

"The present from Arch."

He swallowed hard. He'd returned from the hospital this morning and found a football autographed by Tom Landry and the entire Dallas Cowboys 1977 Super Bowl champion football team on his bed. The card had read, "Happy thirteenth birthday, son. Hope this makes you feel like you're part of the game. Arch."

Patrick had been a rabid Cowboy fan for as long as he could remember. Arch had known. "I found it."

"Arch said he couldn't mail it. There was no way

your mother could pass it off as something she'd bought the way she did with some of the others.''

Great. Another piece of his past buried under lies.

Had Leanna betrayed him? Penny had kept the secret thirty-six years and had nothing to gain by leaking it. Leanna, on the other hand, stood to gain a substantial executrix fee for closing out the estate. The facts spoke for themselves.

So why couldn't he hate her guts the way he ought to?

Because the facts didn't add up. Why would a woman who was in this for the money leave meals in the fridge? Was a guilty conscience enough to keep her from getting in her car and heading back to California?

"Have your gear packed by quitting time. Tonight you're coming home with me."

Patrick sat in the hard-backed chair he'd used since childhood and studied the group gathered around the kitchen table over Sunday morning coffee. Would he lose his right to be here with his brothers when he showed them the letters?

He set the cedar box in the middle of the table. His gaze met Brand's. Brand nodded, showing support Patrick had feared would be missing.

"This box contains love letters written by our mother to Arch Golden. She wrote 'em after their affair." He took a steadying breath. "After she found out she was pregnant with his kid. Me."

Stunned silence greeted his announcement.

"I'm not your brother. Not a Lander."

Brand shook his head. "Yeah, you are."

"Jack's not my father." His throat was so tight he had to force the words out. "I'm Arch Golden's bastard. Crooked Creek is Lander land, and there's no Lander blood in my veins. I don't belong here.''

Caleb laid a hand on his shoulder. ''There's just as much of your blood and sweat out there on the ground as there is of mine.''

Caleb would never know how much his support meant.

Cort snorted. ''Probably more. God knows he's busted more body parts than the rest of us combined. You're one of us, bro, whether you want to be or not. Unless you'd rather be a movie star's son?''

''Hell, no.''

''Then what's your problem?'' Cort asked.

Leanna's announcement had turned his whole life upside down. How could they act like this was unimportant? ''What about Dad?''

Brand set his mug down with a thump. ''You've taken one too many tumbles on your head if you think he's going to feel any differently than *we* do. We'll come with you tonight when you talk to him, if you want.''

If Jack wanted him gone, he didn't want his brothers stuck in the middle. ''I appreciate that, but this is something I'm going to have to do on my own.''

''Where were you last night?''

Leanna nearly jumped out of her skin when she heard Patrick's angry growl. She should have known she'd never get away with hiding from him last night.

Shading her eyes, she glanced over her shoulder and spotted three Lander brothers standing outside the fence. She'd never seen a more intimidating pair than Patrick and Caleb with their arms folded and their poker faces. Cort leaned on the rails beside them, looking substantially less ferocious.

Patrick had called in reinforcements to fire her. She forced a smile even though her nerves stretched tighter than an overwound guitar string. "I'm giving a riding lesson right now. Can we talk later?"

Without waiting for an answer, she turned back to the girl in the round pen. "Sandy, drop your heels down a little more and hold your reining hand steady. Exactly like that. Good."

The gate opened and closed behind her. Footsteps approached and her heart raced. Patrick's cedar and citrus cologne teased her senses and her stomach fluttered. He stopped close enough that she could feel body heat against her back and she had to fight the urge to lean against him.

"Cort will take over. You're coming with me." His voice strummed along her tense nerves. She glanced at him, and his hard expression told her refusing wasn't an option.

She told her student, "Sandy, I'm turning you over to the handsomest cowboy on the spread for the rest of your lesson."

Patrick sucked in a sharp breath beside her. The jealous haze in his eyes sent hope rushing through her veins, but she tamped it down because he still pushed her away at every opportunity—the way everyone did eventually.

Cort, her newest ally, passed her in the gate. He touched the brim of his tan cowboy hat and winked.

Patrick led her to where Caleb waited in the shade and parked his hands on his hips. "You're supposed to wear a hat."

"Who's with Jack?" she countered before Caleb could fire her.

Caleb's piercing assessment made her want to squirm. "Brand. According to the nurses Dad's daughter-in-law has been at the hospital every night, but Brand's wife Toni has been at home with the girls, and my wife's been with me—right up until the minute I put her on a plane this morning."

Busted. She shrugged. "Nights are hard for Jack. He's having trouble with pain management and—"

Patrick muttered a curse. "You're lying to the hospital staff and sneaking in to see Jack? What's the matter? Your conscience bothering you?"

"No. I have nothing to feel guilty about."

"Right." Sarcasm again.

Caleb's eyes narrowed. "I suggested having them toss you out next time you showed up." His expression softened and a new respect entered his eyes. "Dad threatened to leave with you. He swears you're the only reason he's stayed to let the vultures peck on him."

Jack had grumbled those exact words to her this morning before she'd left. She grinned. "I do what I can to help."

Caleb smiled back.

Patrick's gaze jumped from her to Caleb and back. A muscle pulsed in his jaw. "Have you hoodwinked everybody?"

His rejection stung, but surprisingly, she didn't want to drink herself into oblivion the way her mother did when a relationship turned sour. The emotions twisting her insides were painful, but far less destructive. She wanted to comfort Patrick, to be with him, to hold him.

"Apparently not. You're still resisting."

Caleb coughed into his hand, and Leanna saw a sparkle of amusement in his eyes. "I'll let you handle this, bro."

Caleb headed back toward the ranch house without firing her. Leanna released a slow breath.

Patrick took off his hat and shoved a hand through his hair. "Why are you doing this?"

"Because I care about Jack...and I love you." There, she'd said it. Leanna winced when he swallowed hard and looked away. "You don't have to love me back if it scares you."

His spine turned ramrod straight and his gaze pinned her in place. "Leanna..."

She didn't want to hear him say he didn't return her feelings. She hadn't expected him to fall for a mongrel with a screwed-up past and a mother who would always be an issue, but a childish part of her still believed in fairy tales and hoped for a happy ending, a loving family and a man she could trust.

He opened his mouth and she rattled on, "Your mother must have been a special lady to have two wonderful men to love her."

He didn't answer, but the pleat between his brows deepened. Finally he huffed out a breath and shoved his hands into his pockets. "You need to get some sleep instead of spending every night riding the highway between here and San Antonio."

"As long as Jack needs me, I'll be there for him."

"You won't be any good for him or anybody else if you fall asleep behind the wheel and drive your car into a tree."

She wanted to believe that the concern in his eyes meant he cared. "It's not like I'd be missed."

His breath whistled between his teeth. Patrick reached out and grabbed her by the shoulders. "Jack would miss you. Hell, half the crew is already under your spell.'' His eyes darkened and he pulled closer. His gaze drifted to her lips. ''I'd miss you.''

She closed her eyes, tipped her head back, and...waited, but the kiss never happened. He muttered a curse, and the warmth of his hand fell away. She opened her eyes, embarrassment heating her face.

He paced a few steps away. ''Where did you sleep last night? You weren't in the storage building.''

He cared enough to look for her. That had to count for something, didn't it? Or was she spinning fantasies again? She pressed her lips together and refused to answer.

Patrick pulled her yellow ribbon and the house key attached from the front pocket of his jeans. He hung it around her neck and dropped the key down the collar of her shirt. The metal, warmed by his body, hung between her breasts as a reminder of his touch.

''If you don't show up tonight, I'm coming after you. That's not a threat. It's a promise.''

Patrick shoved a hand through his hair and paced the hospital room, waiting—more like dreading—Jack's return from physical therapy.

Leanna was right. He was afraid. Afraid Jack would tell him to pack up and get lost. Terrified the news would cause him to have another heart attack. But no matter how much he dreaded it, he had to broach the subject of his paternity with Jack. He couldn't keep hiding from the truth.

The door opened and a nurse pushed Jack into the room. Patrick did a double take at the snazzy wardrobe.

''What're you staring at?'' Jack waved the nurse off and gingerly levered himself from the wheelchair and shuffled to the bed. She helped him get settled and then left.

"I've never seen you wear pajamas or a bathrobe before."

"Hospital gowns are drafty. Leanna brought these so I wouldn't flash everybody in the hall. The doc makes me walk like some danged Olympian. Need to go home so I can rest."

"Why didn't you tell me Leanna had been sneaking in to see you at night?"

"Figured you'd stop her. That gal needs a daddy. I'm 'bout as close as she's gonna get."

"She's not looking for a father. She's here..." His throat closed up. He paced to the window and back to the bed, racking his brain for the words he'd rehearsed on the way to the hospital.

"Never took you for a coward, boy. Spit it out. And stop circling like a danged buzzard. It's giving me a headache."

He couldn't think of any easy way to say what needed saying. Best to just spit it out. "She's here because of me. I'm not your son."

"Course you are."

"Mom had an affair. Arch Golden is my father."

Jack exhaled slowly and shook his head. "That's where you're wrong. Golden might've planted the seed, but I'm the one who raised you. I'm the one who mopped up your blood and tanned your backside."

Patrick's chest felt tight. He scrambled to make sense of what his father was saying. "How long have you known?"

"Always suspected. Didn't know for sure until after Carolyn died. Letter came. I opened it. It was him. Wanting you."

"Is that why you rode me so hard? Because you resented raising another man's bastard?"

Remorse deepened the lines on Jack's face. "I'll admit I was tougher on you than I was on your brothers, but it was because of your momma, not him. Carolyn spoiled you rotten, and she had you tied to her apron stings so tightly, it's a wonder you didn't strangle. I was afraid she'd turn you into a sissy. Sissies get beaten up. I tried to toughen you up so you could look after yourself in case a time came when I wasn't around."

Patrick swallowed hard and shoved his hand through his hair. "I thought you hated my guts."

Jack grimaced. "That'd be like hating myself, son. Danged if you aren't more like me than any of your brothers. A hell-raising, car-racing, skirt-chasing man, that's for sure. But you got a good heart in you. An' for the right woman, you'll be ready to give all that up for a different kind of excitement. You won't miss it a lick. I never did."

"How can you still love her when she cheated on you?"

"Nobody or nothing is perfect in this life. You have to take the good with the bad and hope the bad don't break you. Most of the fault was mine. I held on to Carolyn too long. I should have let her go, but she wanted to take you boys with her, and I wasn't gonna let that happen. I used every trick in the book to hold on to her."

Patrick cleared his throat, trying to dislodge a knot the size of his boot, and paced back to the window. "She wasn't running off with her lover when she died."

"Leanna read me the letter."

He snapped his head around. She'd read his mother's love letters to another man to Jack? "What?"

"Get the starch out of your shorts. She only reads me the parts that make me sound like some romance book hero. The gal ought to know no man's that perfect."

Amen. "The reporters didn't surprise you?"

"Hell, no. I called 'em. I got so danged nervous 'bout saying I wasn't man enough for my woman that I keeled over."

Leanna hadn't betrayed him, and he'd let her down by not believing her when the chips were down. "Then why call them?"

"Trying to force your hand. I heard you and Leanna talking. Heard you tell her that you were refusing your inheritance because of me. I wanted you to have the money. It would give you chances I couldn't. Ranching has never been your thing. Maybe now you can figure out what is."

His heart stuttered. "Are you throwing me out?"

Jack cackled. "Hell, no. I like having you around to spar with, but that gal has family in California. Visiting Texas is one thing. Moving here's another. And her momma…well, sounds like she ain't a peach, but Leanna stands by her."

The way she'd stood by him. "You're barking up the wrong tree."

"Don't play stupid. Leanna's the best thing that's ever happened to you. But you got to choose. If she wants to go home, are you gonna go with her? Don't make the mistake I did of trying to corral yer woman in a pen where she can't be happy."

Even a blind fool like him could see that Leanna loved the ranch. It was him the shine would wear off of as soon as she lost her rose-colored glasses. "She's too young for me. Hell, she's younger than Cort."

"Are you worried you won't be able to satisfy her—in bed, I mean."

He whipped his head toward Jack so fast he'd probably have a permanent crick in his neck. Heat scorched his cheeks. Sex was one topic they'd never discussed. "Hell, no."

"Then what's your problem? She's nuts about you."

"She deserves somebody better than me—somebody who can live up to that superhero image Mom created."

Jack shook his head. "Son, you're wrong on both counts there. Your momma called it like she saw it. You're a rebel, but you're honest as an August day is long, and you've always put your family first. That's why Caleb knew he could call on you and why Brand trusts you with those girls."

Jack stood and hobbled to the window to stand beside him. "As to t'other. What's the one thing you know how to do better than anybody else?"

"Screw up?"

Jack chuckled. "You've made your share of mistakes, I'll grant you that. What I'm talking about is that you know how to have fun better than anybody I know." He laid a hand on Patrick's shoulder. "Son, I've never met anybody who needed to learn to play more than Leanna.

"If you love her, go after her with all you've got, but remember, sacrifice cuts both ways. I made your mother do all the giving. We both know how that turned out."

Patrick's heart thumped against his ribs. Could he be

the man Leanna needed? Did he dare risk her breaking his heart? Hadn't she already?

But could he give up his home and family and move halfway across the country for her?

Ten

Patrick stomped into Red Dog's Wednesday night with one goal on his mind—to drink himself into oblivion.

He crossed the smoky room without acknowledging his friends and slid his keys across the bar to the bartender. "Riley, don't give 'em back tonight no matter what I say or do."

"Jack's doing well. You must be having woman troubles."

"Yeah. Pass me a shot glass and keep pouring."

Riley brought out a bottle of tequila, filled a shot glass and set it in front of him.

Patrick tossed back the first shot and winced when the liquor burned a trail all the way to the soles of his boots.

He wanted Leanna for keeps, but he couldn't have her. If he married her he'd have to give up his home and family or ask her to give up hers. His life was proof that either was a no-win situation. He'd racked his brain trying to come up with a compromise and couldn't.

Hell, it didn't matter. Even if he could work out a solution she'd probably never forgive him for turning on her like a rabid dog anyway.

Riley refilled his glass. "Who's picking you up?"

"Don't know, and in a few minutes I won't care."

Ava waltzed up and draped herself over his back. Her ample breasts pressed into his shoulderblades and *nothing happened.* No zap. No zing. Not a speck of interest.

A sure sign Leanna had him roped, tied and branded.

"Hi, handsome. Can I join you?" she breathed into his ear.

He'd spent time dancing with the redhead, vertically and horizontally, but his tastes these days ran to gals with light-brown, sun-streaked hair, baggy clothes and sassy smiles. "Not tonight, darlin'. This is a one-man pity party."

She pouted prettily, but wandered off when he knocked back another shot. The second didn't bite nearly as bad as the first.

Riley shoved a bowl of peanuts at him. "Anybody I know?"

"Nope."

"She have anything to do with the reporters in town?"

"Yeah." The third shot barely stung his throat at all.

Somebody brushed against him, and for a second he thought Ava had come back, but then he smelled Leanna's sunshine and vanilla scent and his brain dropped to his shorts—a familiar place these days.

The woman had driven him to hallucinating. No way would she come to a dive like Red Dog's.

Cort settled on the stool to his right. "I don't want to be you tomorrow."

"Me, neither."

Cort rapped his knuckles on the bar. "Hey, Riley, how about drawing us a round of beers?"

A round? Patrick turned in time to see Leanna settle on the stool between Cort's and Caleb's. She didn't even glance his way.

Couldn't a man get drunk in peace? "Gimme my keys, Riley."

"No sirree."

He'd walk home rather than sit here and let the emptiness in his chest swallow him whole. Every time he looked at Leanna, the fact that he'd let her down punched him in the gut.

Patrick stood and reached for his wallet. His back pocket was empty. He patted his other pocket, even searched the pockets of his jean jacket. Nothing but lint. "Put it on my tab."

"You know danged well I don't run tabs. Pay before you go or you'll sleep in the jail."

"I left my wallet at home." He was pretty damned certain he hadn't, but the liquor had hit his empty stomach and his memory was getting a little fuzzy.

He thought he saw Cort smirk. "Cort'll cover me."

"Sorry, bro. No can do. I'm broke."

Caleb headed for the jukebox before Patrick could ask and he danged sure wouldn't ask Leanna to pay his tab. Hell, she was the reason he was here. Just looking at her wrenched his heart. He loved her, but she deserved a helluva lot more than he could offer. And then of course there was that little matter of him screwing up royally by not trusting her.

One of his buddies came up and asked her to dance. Damned if she didn't follow the jerk out onto the floor.

Clenching his fist, he debated knocking Sam's teeth down his throat but sat back down. "Why'd you bring her?"

Cort shrugged. "She got a phone call. It seemed to upset her. I thought getting out might do her some good."

His gaze darted back to Leanna. She sure didn't look upset when she smiled at Sam that way. He ground his teeth against the urge to go to her.

"Might as well quit pulling on the line. She has you hooked."

He muttered an obscenity to Cort and followed it with the appropriate hand gesture in case his brother couldn't hear over the jukebox wailing a song about the woman who got away and the fool who'd let her go.

Cort just laughed. "I'll help you pick out a ring before I head back to school."

"Won't be buying a ring." He ignored his liquor and watched Leanna dance. The woman sure knew how to move. His blood pressure kicked up a notch with every wiggle of her hips in those baggy britches.

Caleb returned. "I can't believe you'd let her dance with Sam. Gals say he has more tentacles than an octopus."

The tequila burned his belly. He sure as hell wasn't jealous. All right, so maybe he was, but this was put-up-or-shut-up time. He couldn't offer her forever and even if he could she'd probably tell him where to shove it. He had to let her go, but damned if it didn't hurt.

He rubbed his chest. "I don't have the right to stop her."

Caleb snorted. "She's sleeping with you. That's a damned good reason to object."

"Do you love her?" Cort asked.

"Doesn't matter. I can't give her what she needs. Even if I could, she wouldn't want it from me."

"Come again?" Caleb asked over the top of his beer.

"What if she wants to move back to California? I don't want to leave the ranch, and I don't know what in the hell I'd do out in Hollywood. Don't care who fathered me, I'm no actor."

Caleb's heavy mug hit the bar with a thump. "That's a load of bull. If you love her, you go where she goes and you do it on your knees if you have to. Otherwise, you'll be spending all your time at Red Dog's, and Riley will start to look pretty."

Riley made an obscene gesture.

Caleb downed his beer.

Cort shrugged. "I don't see your problem. I live half way across the country. It doesn't make me any less family does it? Home's not a place, you ignoramus. It's the people. Mr. Millionaire, you can afford to fly back and forth whenever the mood strikes you."

Caleb pulled out his wallet and laid a bill on the bar. "Forget it, Cort. He's just being stupid. This isn't about where he hangs his hat. Is it, Patrick?"

His brother's gaze pinned him down until he broke the connection and took another look at the woman he loved. The tightness in his chest increased. "I guess you think that because you're married you know all about this relationship business."

"I know enough to recognize fear when I smell it."

Cort, hearing the insult, stepped out of the way. God knows he and Caleb had fought over less accurate insults before, but Patrick didn't punch Caleb for calling him a coward. He could hardly take offense at the truth.

He fiddled with the shot glass. "I let her down. When the chips hit the fan I didn't trust her."

"Bingo. So what are you going to do about it? Sit here and cry in your tequila? Or beg her to overlook your stupidity?" Caleb stood. "Give me your keys. I'm taking your truck."

Riley shoved his keys across the bar.

"When you get through feeling sorry for yourself, ask nicely and maybe Leanna will give you a ride home."

Cort slapped Patrick's shoulder. "Trust me, bro, this one's a keeper. As a matter of fact, if you throw her back, I might just have to go fishing for her, myself."

Patrick took a swing at him, but Cort dodged his fist and laughed all the way out of the building on Caleb's heels.

His gaze ricocheted back to Leanna. Did he love her? Without a doubt. But did she love him enough to forgive him for being an ass? He rubbed the back of his neck.

Could he stand to see Sam—or any other jerk for that matter—putting the moves on her? Hell, no.

Could he let her go back to California without him? The knot in his gut was all the answer he needed. If she'd forgive him they could have houses in both places. Hell, he was a freaking millionaire. He could afford it.

"Riley, call Penny for me and tell her I'll need room ten for the night."

Shoving away from the bar, he marched across the

room, cut through the dancers on the floor and tapped Sam on the shoulder. "Cutting in."

Sam swung Leanna away. "Get your own woman."

"She *is* mine."

Leanna stopped so fast Sam nearly ran over her. Her wide-eyed gaze locked with his and it didn't look like hatred in her greeny-gold eyes.

"Tell Sam to let you go, angel, before I hit him."

She wet her lips, took a shaky breath and then pulled her hands from her partner's. "Thanks for the dance."

Sam scowled but left the floor.

Patrick offered his hand. The touch of her palm on his sizzled through his veins like a lit fuse on dynamite. He pulled her into his arms and held her tight, savoring her scent and the feel of her pressed against him and taking comfort in the fact that she didn't knee him in the groin, stomp his instep or poke his eyes out.

Could he handle a lifetime of her body next to his? No doubt about it.

"Patrick. The song's over."

So it was, and way too soon for his liking. He had some serious groveling to do. The floor emptied. Reluctantly he released her but kept hold of her hand and led her off the floor and toward the door. "I'd offer you a drink, but I don't have my wallet."

"It's in my purse. I picked your pocket when we came in."

He stopped in his tracks. "Do I want to know where you picked up that skill?"

She grinned and wrinkled her nose in that adorable way that made him want to kiss her until she whimpered. "Actually, I've never picked anybody's pocket before, but it seemed like a good way to keep you here."

That sounded good. He held the door open and followed her outside into the moonlight. "Why do you need to keep me here?"

She averted her gaze and swallowed. "To say goodbye."

His insides were knotted so tightly he'd probably rupture something. Her station wagon was parked in front of the bar, but he walked right past it, leading her toward the rooming house two blocks away.

"Where are we going?"

"The Palace. I...we need to talk." How could he convince her to give him another shot? And then the idea hit him. He'd call in the big guns. He stopped under a streetlight and met her gaze. "I don't want you to go."

"Patrick—"

He saw the doubt in her eyes and interrupted before she could shoot him down. "I asked Penny about your ghost. She says Annabel wraps true lovers in a blanket of warmth. The rest of 'em she freezes." He cupped her shoulders in his hands. "I felt her. Annabel, that is, not Penny."

Excitement and wariness flickered in Leanna's eyes. She grabbed his jacket in both hands. "Was she warm or cold?"

A ray of hope warmed his heart when she didn't tell him to kiss off. Despite the kinks in his belly, he winked and bent until their foreheads touched. "That's for me to know and you to find out. And, angel, I promise you're gonna love finding out."

He pulled her into his arms and kissed her until the fit of his jeans made walking the rest of the way to the Palace an iffy proposition. Reluctantly, he released her and ordered his boots to move before he changed his mind and pulled her behind Mrs. Lee's lilac bushes.

Penny opened the door before he knocked and pressed the key into his hand. "Go on up. If Leanna's staying with you tonight then I'm going to stay with Jack. The rest of the house is empty, so lock up when you leave if I'm not back. Kitchen's stocked. Help yourself."

Without another word, she climbed into her car and left.

Leanna tried to catch her breath as Patrick hustled her up the stairs and into room ten. He ushered her to the chair, nudged her to sit down and dropped to one knee. Her heart skipped a beat.

Was that love shining in his dark eyes? Had he finally realized she hadn't called the press?

"I want to spend the rest of my life ghost-hunting with you."

He couldn't mean what she hoped.

"We can do that in Texas or back in California if you need to be near your momma."

Leanna's happiness dimmed. "Tonya might not be in California. She called earlier today to tell me she's made a major breakthrough, and that she's moving home to Georgia to be with my father."

"Does he know this?"

"He's the one who signed her out of rehab. Somehow she got to a phone and called him. He flew out to pick her up this morning."

"Have you ever met him—your father?"

"Once. He threatened to call the police if I didn't leave." She gripped his hands. "Patrick, what will I do if she's wrong? What if she goes off the deep end again?"

He cupped the back of her neck and tipped up her chin with his thumb. "The one thing I've learned from all this is that we're not responsible for our parents' mistakes, but if Tonya needs us, then we'll be there for her."

"*We?* You don't have to—"

He hushed her with a gentle kiss. "Yeah, I do. I love you, and loving you means we're in this together."

The words she wanted so badly to hear were bittersweet. "You didn't trust me, Patrick, and that hurt."

He grimaced. "I know and I'm sorrier than I can say. I screwed up. You've bent over backward to help me and my family, and I turned on you, but if you forgive me, I guarantee I'll do my best to never let you down again."

A muscle in his jaw twitched. "Leanna, you've got to believe that no man will ever love you the way I do. I'm an idiot, but I'm the only idiot for you. Marry me and let me take care of you. I promise I'll make sure the rest of your life is a helluva lot more fun than the first part."

Her heart soared like a helium balloon, but reality kept her tethered. Heros only settled for heroines, and she was the mongrel daughter of a forgettable woman. She took a deep breath and stroked her fingers across his bristly jaw.

"I'm not a stray who needs a home. Although it seems that you and both of your fathers seem to think so."

He frowned. "Is that a yes or a no?"

"Patrick, what if this is just the tequila talking, or if you've been without a woman or Red Dog's for so long that even *I* look good? I don't expect you to love me. I'm just not…lovable.''

He shot to his feet and stared down at her as if she'd lost her mind. "Where'd you get that crazy idea?"

"Everyone I've ever grown attached to has found it easy to forget me. I'm afraid you will, too."

Frustration flared in his eyes. "If you want proof that I'm in this for the long haul, I'll get your name tattooed on my butt."

He strode to the door, muttering under his breath about women and their danged fool notions. He dropped the key and kicked it through the narrow gap between the door and the floor. It slid into the hall, out of sight and out of reach. She didn't bother to tell him how easy the skeleton lock would be to pick.

He turned and parked his hands on his hips. "I admitted I was stupid, but I'm not dumb enough to let you walk out of my life. I guess I'll have to keep you here until Annabel and I can convince you that we belong together."

The temperature in the room rose a few degrees, but it had more to do with the wicked promise in his eyes than the presence of any supernatural spirits. As many ghost stories as she and Arch had investigated, not one had ever proven true. Evidently, ghosts, like fairy tales, were just a figment of someone's overactive imagination.

He crossed the room, stretched out on the bed, and folded his arms behind his head. "If we get the license tomorrow then the seventy-two-hour waiting period will be up by the time Dad comes home from the hospital. We can have the ceremony on Crooked Creek, and since Dad has taken a shine to you, he'd probably like to walk you down the aisle."

Her heart fluttered at the image he painted. "Patrick—"

"I'll muster the troops. Toni and Brooke should be able to throw together a wedding in three days."

"But—"

He kept right on planning, as if her acceptance was guaranteed. "We can honeymoon right here at the Palace or in Hollywood, if you want to show me Arch's place."

"Carlsbad. Arch's estate is in Carlsbad, not Hollywood."

"Wherever. It's not the place I'm interested in." He waggled his brows and patted the bed. "Come sit down and tell me about…my father."

She put a hand to her chest, and her eyes stung. She knew how hard it was for him to ask. "I still have his letter to you in my purse."

Patrick swallowed hard and took a deep breath. "I guess it's time I read it."

She found the sealed envelope and handed it to him. He slid his finger beneath the flap. She turned to give him privacy, but he caught her hand. "Have you read this?"

"No."

He pulled her onto the bed beside him, tucking her head against his shoulder and aligning her body with his. Despite his casual posture, every muscle in his body was as hard as stone against her. He cleared his throat and pulled the two heavy sheets of stationery from the envelope. He read aloud:

"Dear Son,
If you're reading this, then I guess I never found the courage to introduce myself. You need to

know that I'm proud of you. You've turned into the man your mother always promised you'd become. As much as I hate to admit it, I have to give the credit to Jack Lander, because I wasn't there for you. I regret that more than you'll ever know, but Carolyn was right. You had a home and a family and I didn't have the right to take those away from you. But don't believe that I forgot about you for one single day.

I'm leaving my estate to you, not because I want to buy your forgiveness, but because lack of money is what made me leave your mother behind. I don't want you to have to make those tough choices.

You were always in my heart, son. My only regret is that I didn't have the courage to have you in my life.''

Patrick folded the letter and tossed it on the bedside table. He exhaled slowly.

Leanna tightened her arms around him. ''You're a very lucky man to have two fathers and a mother who loved you.''

His lips touched her hair. ''I'll love you enough to make up for what you missed.''

Tears sprang to her eyes. She wanted to say yes with all her heart, but what if he changed his mind?

He traced a tantalizing pattern along her spine and then tunneled his fingers beneath her T-shirt to caress her back, her hip, her waist. He nuzzled her neck, nibbled her ear and a shudder raced through her. His fingertips traced an ever-widening pattern of circles around her navel until he brushed the underside of her breasts and the sensitive skin between her legs.

She bit her lip to stifle a cry when he plucked at her nipple through the thin fabric of her bra. "Patrick—"

"Shh. Let me love you." Her bra snapped open, and his hands closed over her bared breasts.

"I can't think when you do that."

"Then this'll really mess you up." She felt him smile against her temple seconds before his fingers dipped beneath the drawstring of her pants.

"I like teaching you new things," he said in a voice as smooth as black velvet. His tongue delved into her ear at the same instant his fingers found her wetness and slicked a trail over her most sensitive spot.

A moan burst from her lips and every muscle in her body tensed in anticipation. "I can't…"

"Yes, you can." His magical fingers diligently plied her until she shattered in his arms. He withdrew his hand, kissed her hard and stood her up beside the bed while her knees were still quaking. The look he gave her would tempt a nun to sin. "Last one naked is on the bottom."

She'd never been one to strip in a hurry, but after only a second's hesitation, Leanna shucked her shirt, pants and panties. Patrick was still tugging off his jeans when she climbed back onto the bed and hugged her knees to her chest.

"That would be you, cowboy."

He looked far from disappointed. "Angel, you're in for the ride of your life."

Heat and anticipation prickled her skin.

He wore only a condom when he pulled her into his arms and soldered their lips in a kiss as carnal and primitive as the need building inside her. With a quick twist he rolled over, shifting her until she straddled his hips. His fingers combed through her hair, lingering where tendrils draped her breasts until she whimpered.

"Take me inside, Leanna."

She positioned herself above him and then lowered until his thickness pushed a moan from her throat. His slightly roughened palms scraped a path from her hips to her breasts, around her shoulders and down her back, stirring her senses into a whirl. Cupping her bottom, he demonstrated a rhythm guaranteed to drive her wild.

Tension and heat coiled tighter in her midsection. Patrick surrounded her, filled her. He feasted on her lips, her jaw, her neck. She arched back, gasping from the overload of sensations, and he captured her breast in his scalding mouth. Leanna rode faster, chasing the white-hot need until she caught it and soared like a comet. Her cry mingled with Patrick's groan as he bowed up to meet her in one last shuddering thrust.

She collapsed into a boneless heap across his heaving chest. He tightened his arms around her, making her wish this interlude in Texas didn't have to end, but it would just like every other relationship in her life unless she found the courage to risk loving him.

She'd spent her life running. It was time to stop. Loving Patrick had taught her one very important lesson. She wasn't her mother. She wouldn't self-destruct if their relationship hit a rough spot. And what relationship never did? She didn't want to regret not having the courage to have Patrick in her life.

Patrick nuzzled her brow and then tipped up her chin. The love in his eyes was as clear and bright as the crystal chandelier hanging in Arch's mansion. "Marry me, Leanna. You've shown me what it's like to be loved. Let me show you."

The air stirred, wrapping them in a cocoon of warmth.

Goose bumps rose on Leanna's skin. She pressed herself against Patrick's chest and clutched him tighter. Was this Annabel? ''Patrick?''

''Don't tell me you're scared?'' He outlined her face with kisses and sipped at her lips. The room grew warmer—or maybe it was just her.

''Of course not.'' She swallowed hard.

''I don't mean of the ghost.'' He lifted her away just enough to meet her gaze. ''I mean of us. I dare you to give me the chance to prove I can be the man you think I am.''

Competitive spirit surged in her blood. ''Haven't you learned not to challenge me yet, cowboy?''

He shrugged. ''You got lucky a couple of times, but luck won't always be on your side.''

''You're wrong. I'm the luckiest woman on the planet because I found my hero.'' Leanna cupped his cheek. ''I love you, Patrick.''

His eyes softened. He stroked her hair back from her face with a tender, unsteady hand. ''I love you, too.''

He flipped her over and she found herself flat on her back with Patrick pinning her to the mattress. ''Now, tell me, is that a yes? Because I'm not willing to take no for an answer.''

The happiness inside her swelled until it bubbled over in a laugh. ''That, cowboy, is most definitely a yes.''

Epilogue

The noose around his neck was about to choke him.

Patrick looked down into his bride's shining eyes, but the tightness in his throat wasn't caused by his fancy neckwear. It was love—the one emotion he'd planned to avoid. Good thing he'd screwed that up.

He grinned and slid his gaze from the ring of pearls in Leanna's hair, over the thin pearl straps on her bare, flushed shoulders to the yards and yards of floaty stuff in the skirt. She looked like a princess in the wedding dress his sister-in-law had helped her pick out. He couldn't wait to strip her right out of everything except the matching gold rings glittering on her finger and her toe.

"How long do I have to wear this danged tie?"

She had on her I've-got-a-secret smile. "Not much longer. We're not leaving until I give you one more present from Arch. I told you I saved the best for last, didn't I?'' So she had. Leanna pulled on his hand before he could ask questions. ''I need to thank Brooke and Toni for all their help.''

His sisters-in-law must have bought every hanging basket from here to Hawaii. He couldn't walk around the porch without whacking his head on one, but he'd gladly take a few knocks on the noggin to see Leanna's face light up the way it had when they'd started unloading the flowers.

Leanna towed him through the wedding guests toward the gathering around the punch bowl. His gaze landed on the dozens of satin-covered buttons down the back of her dress, and his fingers tingled in anticipation of releasing them.

Brooke stepped forward and hugged Leanna. ''I was about to come and get you. I want to make you an offer I hope you won't refuse. Caleb and I would like you to consider accepting the job of dude ranch hostess permanently once you return from your honeymoon. It will give me more time to develop the motivational side of the business and to deal with junior.'' She patted her belly.

Leanna's dazzling smile nearly knocked him off his feet. ''I'd love it.''

''Wish finding a dude ranch manager was that easy,'' Caleb grumbled beside her.

Leanna glanced his way and then back to his brother. ''Have you considered asking Patrick? He loves the dude ranch.''

Caleb's gaze lasered in on him. ''Would you be willing?''

''Hell, yes, if you'd handle Crooked Creek.''

''Deal.'' They shook on it.

A car door slammed and Leanna stiffened beside

him. Her fingers squeezed his so tight he figured he had a case of gangrene in his future.

A woman teetered across the lawn in impossibly high heels. "Leanna! Oh, baby, I can't believe you got married without us." She pulled Leanna into her arms and hugged her.

Leanna stood stiff as a fence post. She didn't hug back. "Tonya."

His mother-in-law, and most likely the man trailing behind her like a dog with his tail between his legs was Leanna's father. Patrick's hackles rose. These folks had given his bride a world of hurt. That stopped now.

"Why didn't you tell me you were getting married?"

"I didn't know where to find you. You're AWOL from the clinic."

"Oh, that. I had a major breakthrough with this new doctor. I finally figured out that I never quit loving your father. All the men I've lived with in the past few years were just attempts to replace him. Each relationship was destined to fail because the men weren't Harland. I used alcohol and drugs to dull the disappointment, but I've been clean for the past month and I plan to stay that way."

The man stepped forward, hooking his hand around Tonya's waist. "I'll make damn sure of it. And I owe you an apology, Leanna. When you came to visit me, I was in the middle of a nasty divorce. I was afraid that having you show up would jeopardize custody of my girls, and I turned you away."

The sound of a car horn drew Patrick's attention. His jaw dropped when he spotted the cherry-red '67 Mustang convertible coming up the driveway. He whipped his head around to Leanna.

She smiled and turned back to her mother. "Tonya, I wish you and Harland the best of luck. Please excuse us."

Leanna led him to the end of the sidewalk and handed him an envelope. He ripped it open and recognized Arch's handwriting. "Happy sixteenth birthday, son." It was dated the day he'd turned sixteen.

Arch might not have been there physically, but he'd been there. Love evidently came in many forms.

Cort parked the car beside them, climbed out and tossed the keys to Patrick.

He caught them. "You're next, little brother."

Cort shook his head. "No way, nothing is going to come between me and my surgical training."

Jack ambled around the car and stopped beside them. "Suitcases are in the trunk. We'll pick up the car later from the airport." Jack swallowed hard. "You'll come back?"

Patrick heard the tension in his voice. "I'll be back."

"You might like it out there. A mansion, for gosh sakes."

"Doesn't matter. My family's here."

"Fancy cars and servants. I'd understand if—"

"Dad…" Patrick hugged him for the first time in his life. "We'll see you next week."

Without another word he swept Leanna off her feet, circled the car and set her in the passenger seat.

Leanna looked at him and smiled. "I guess true love never dies."

Patrick climbed in beside her and winked. "That's what I've been trying to tell you, angel. Does this mean I don't need the tattoo?"

Leanna's low and sexy laugh stirred his insides like

a shaken beehive. "I kind of like the idea of knowing I'm under your skin."

"Trust me, angel, you're already there."

She looped her arms around his neck and opened her mouth over his in a kiss so carnal he nearly burst a blood vessel.

By the time he put the car in gear they were both breathing hard. The ghosts from their pasts were settled. Now he and his bride could concentrate on the future.

*   *   *   *   *

If you enjoyed what you just read,
then we've got an offer you can't resist!

Take 2 bestselling love stories FREE!

Plus get a FREE surprise gift!

Clip this page and mail it to Silhouette Reader Service™

IN U.S.A.	IN CANADA
3010 Walden Ave.	P.O. Box 609
P.O. Box 1867	Fort Erie, Ontario
Buffalo, N.Y. 14240-1867	L2A 5X3

YES! Please send me 2 free Silhouette Desire® novels and my free surprise gift. After receiving them, if I don't wish to receive anymore, I can return the shipping statement marked cancel. If I don't cancel, I will receive 6 brand-new novels every month, before they're available in stores! In the U.S.A., bill me at the bargain price of $3.57 plus 25¢ shipping and handling per book and applicable sales tax, if any*. In Canada, bill me at the bargain price of $4.24 plus 25¢ shipping and handling per book and applicable taxes**. That's the complete price and a savings of at least 10% off the cover prices—what a great deal! I understand that accepting the 2 free books and gift places me under no obligation ever to buy any books. I can always return a shipment and cancel at any time. Even if I never buy another book from Silhouette, the 2 free books and gift are mine to keep forever.

225 SDN DNUP
326 SDN DNUQ

Name	(PLEASE PRINT)	
Address	Apt.#	
City	State/Prov.	Zip/Postal Code

* Terms and prices subject to change without notice. Sales tax applicable in N.Y.
** Canadian residents will be charged applicable provincial taxes and GST.
All orders subject to approval. Offer limited to one per household and not valid to current Silhouette Desire® subscribers.
® are registered trademarks of Harlequin Books S.A., used under license.

DES02   ©1998 Harlequin Enterprises Limited

Your opinion is important to us! Please take a few moments to share your thoughts with us about your experiences with Harlequin and Silhouette books. Your comments will be very useful in ensuring that we deliver books you love to read. *Please take a few minutes to complete the questionnaire, then send it to us at the address below.*

Send your completed questionnaires to:
Harlequin/Silhouette Reader Survey, P.O. Box 9046, Buffalo, NY 14269-9046

1. As you may know, there are many different lines under the Harlequin and Silhouette brands. Each of the lines is listed below. Please check the box that most represents your reading habit for each line.

Line	Currently read this line	Do not read this line	Not sure if I read this line
Harlequin American Romance	❑	❑	❑
Harlequin Duets	❑	❑	❑
Harlequin Romance	❑	❑	❑
Harlequin Historicals	❑	❑	❑
Harlequin Superromance	❑	❑	❑
Harlequin Intrigue	❑	❑	❑
Harlequin Presents	❑	❑	❑
Harlequin Temptation	❑	❑	❑
Harlequin Blaze	❑	❑	❑
Silhouette Special Edition	❑	❑	❑
Silhouette Romance	❑	❑	❑
Silhouette Intimate Moments	❑	❑	❑
Silhouette Desire	❑	❑	❑

2. Which of the following best describes why you bought *this book?* One answer only, please.

the picture on the cover	❑	the title	❑
the author	❑	the line is one I read often	❑
part of a miniseries	❑	saw an ad in another book	❑
saw an ad in a magazine/newsletter	❑	a friend told me about it	❑
I borrowed/was given this book	❑	other: _____	❑

3. Where did you buy *this book?* One answer only, please.

at Barnes & Noble	❑	at a grocery store	❑
at Waldenbooks	❑	at a drugstore	❑
at Borders	❑	on eHarlequin.com Web site	❑
at another bookstore	❑	from another Web site	❑
at Wal-Mart	❑	Harlequin/Silhouette Reader	❑
at Target	❑	Service/through the mail	
at Kmart	❑	used books from anywhere	❑
at another department store or mass merchandiser	❑	I borrowed/was given this book	❑

4. On average, how many Harlequin and Silhouette books do you buy at one time?

I buy _____ books at one time	❑
I rarely buy a book	❑

MRQ403SD-1A

5. How many times per month do you shop for any *Harlequin and/or Silhouette* books?
   One answer only, please.

1 or more times a week	❑	a few times per year	❑
1 to 3 times per month	❑	less often than once a year	❑
1 to 2 times every 3 months	❑	never	❑

6. When you think of your ideal heroine, which *one* statement describes her the best?
   One answer only, please.

She's a woman who is strong-willed	❑	She's a desirable woman	❑
She's a woman who is needed by others	❑	She's a powerful woman	❑
She's a woman who is taken care of	❑	She's a passionate woman	❑
She's an adventurous woman	❑	She's a sensitive woman	❑

7. The following statements describe types or genres of books that you may be
   interested in reading. Pick *up to 2 types* of books that you are most interested in.

I like to read about truly romantic relationships	❑
I like to read stories that are sexy romances	❑
I like to read romantic comedies	❑
I like to read a romantic mystery/suspense	❑
I like to read about romantic adventures	❑
I like to read romance stories that involve family	❑
I like to read about a romance in times or places that I have never seen	❑
Other: _____	❑

*The following questions help us to group your answers with those readers who are
similar to you. Your answers will remain confidential.*

8. Please record your year of birth below.
   19 _____

9. What is your marital status?
   single ❑   married ❑   common-law ❑   widowed ❑
   divorced/separated ❑

10. Do you have children 18 years of age or younger currently living at home?
    yes ❑   no ❑

11. Which of the following best describes your employment status?
    employed full-time or part-time ❑   homemaker ❑   student ❑
    retired ❑   unemployed ❑

12. Do you have access to the Internet from either home or work?
    yes ❑   no ❑

13. Have you ever visited eHarlequin.com?
    yes ❑   no ❑

14. What state do you live in?
    _____

15. Are you a member of Harlequin/Silhouette Reader Service?
    yes ❑   Account # _____   no ❑   MRQ403SD-1B